Broken Mountain Man

A Stuck Together Protector Romance

Stevie Fox

Copyright © 2024 by Stevie Fox

All rights reserved.

No part of this publication may be reproduced, distributed, or transmitted in any form or by any means, including photocopying, recording, or other electronic or mechanical methods, without the prior written permission of the publisher, except as permitted by U.S. copyright law. For permission requests, contact info@steviefoxauthor.com.

The story, all names, characters, and incidents portrayed in this production are fictitious. No identification with actual persons (living or deceased), places, buildings, and products is intended or should be inferred.

Contents

Introduction	V
1. Logan	1
2. Elena	10
3. Logan	19
4. Elena	28
5. Logan	38
6. Elena	49
7. Logan	59
8. Elena	68
9. Logan	82
10. Elena	92
11. Logan	101
12. Elena	112
13. Logan	123
14. Elena	131

15.	Logan	139
16.	Elena	148
17.	Logan	159
18.	Elena	167
19.	Logan	178
Epilogue - Elena		187
Sneak Peek		199

Introduction

Who's the rugged man with the smouldering eyes?

Oh great...

I'm stranded in the wilderness with an ex-military alpha.

I want to shout Help, but also... Yum!

Finding myself lost and stranded wasn't part of my plan.

Yet, there he is, my rescuer, with biceps bigger than my problems.

A gruff exterior that screams 'stay away.'

But I can't, we're stuck in the wilderness together.

Every touch, every glance sets my skin on fire.

I've never felt this way before, so alive, so tempted.

This commanding protector is making me want more than just to be rescued.

If only I could keep this secret growing in my belly...

1

Logan

Danger lurked in every part of this forest, but that was fine for four reasons: I was accustomed to danger, I knew how to navigate my way around it, I was all alone, and it was safer for everyone else who always seemed to be in danger when I was around.

After all, I'm a curse to them, for it seems I'm the magnet that draws danger's ire, leaving everyone scathed in my wake while I remain unscathed.

The air was thick with the scent of pine and damp earth, mingling with the faint aroma of wood smoke from the chimney of my cabin. It was a scent that had become as familiar to me as the sound of my own heartbeat, a constant reminder of my solitary existence in this vast wilderness.

As I prowled through the underbrush, I kept my senses finely tuned to my surroundings. The forest always seemed to come alive in the evening, toward night, and it had become my favorite time to hunt.

With the chirping of crickets and the occasional hoot of an owl echoing through the trees, each sound was a potential threat, even though I'd become accustomed to moving with the stealth and precision of a predator stalking its prey.

The darkness seemed to close in around me, the shadows dancing and shifting with every flicker of fading light that filtered through the dense canopy above. I knew that danger could lurk behind every tree, every shadow, so I remained hyper-vigilant, my senses tingling with anticipation.

Suddenly, a twig snapped underfoot, the sound echoing like a gunshot in the stillness of the night. My heart leaped into my throat as I whipped around, rifle at the ready, scanning the darkness for any sign of movement.

But the forest remained silent, save for the gentle rustle of leaves in the breeze. I breathed a sigh of relief, the tension slowly draining from my body as I realized it was just a harmless woodland creature scurrying through the underbrush in search of its next meal.

Even as I relaxed, I knew that I could never truly let my guard down in these woods. For in the wilderness, danger lurked around every corner, and survival depended on staying one step ahead of the unknown.

A lump and slight movement caught my eye as I continued moving, almost an unnoticeable shift in the darkness beyond the trees. Instinctively, I raised my rifle again, its familiar weight a comforting presence in my hands.

As I scanned the area with practiced precision, every muscle in my body tensed, ready to spring into action at the first sign of danger. And then, among the shadows, I spotted her: an unmoving figure.

Her form was barely discernible against the backdrop of darkness. My heart quickened its pace, a drumbeat echoing in my chest as I approached cautiously, the undergrowth rustling beneath my feet.

I raced toward the unconscious figure when I sensed no danger was present; my heart thundered in my chest, the adrenaline coursing through my veins like wildfire. But as I closed the distance, the scene that greeted me halted me in my tracks.

A whirlwind of chaos amidst the serene embrace of the forest, the details of her appearance began to emerge as I drew close, like a painting gradually coming into focus. Her hair, tousled and tangled with leaves and twigs, framed a face as pale as moonlight, her features serene in their unconscious repose.

She lay there, trapped in one of my hunting traps, her leg ensnared in its unforgiving grip. Blood pooled around her legs, a stark contrast against the verdant undergrowth beneath her.

A surge of panic threatened to overwhelm me as I knelt beside her, but I knew time was of the essence; she'd already lost too much blood. I could tell just by looking at her pale, unconscious face.

Something within me stirred, and I struggled not to lose control. I wondered if my tendency to place people in danger had affected her just because she came into the forest. I shook my head, unwilling to believe or succumb to the thought.

With a sense of purpose that bordered on obsession to save her, I set to work, tearing makeshift bandages from scraps of my clothes that would be used to bind her wounds and try to staunch the bleeding.

I knelt beside her, and with steady hands, I reached for the hunting trap, my fingers tracing the cold metal with practiced ease. Gently, I began to pry apart its jaws, each movement a silent prayer for her safety.

The trap yielded reluctantly, its grip loosening inch by agonizing inch as I worked to free her from its clutches. With a final, desperate tug, the mechanism released its hold, and I breathed a sigh of relief as her leg emerged, bloodied and deeply injured but mercifully intact.

With careful precision, I began to assess the extent of her injuries, my fingers probing gently for broken bones and torn flesh. With each discovery, my heart sank a little lower; she would have a very slow recovery.

Using the torn strips of cloth I had set aside, I fashioned makeshift bandages and splints, my hands moving with a sense of urgency born of desperation. Each touch was infused with a silent plea for her to hold on, to find the strength to fight against the darkness that threatened to consume her.

I could feel the weight of her vulnerability pressing down on me, threatening to overwhelm me with its magnitude. But

I pushed aside my own fears and doubts, focusing all my energy on the task at hand.

Hours seemed to pass in a blur as I tended to her wounds, the forest around us growing even darker and silent as night fell. But still, I pressed on, refusing to give in to the exhaustion that tugged at me.

And then, finally, it was done. She lay before me, her injuries bound and bandaged as best I could manage with the limited resources at my disposal. I leaned down to hold a finger over her neck to be sure she had a heartbeat and was still breathing.

I reached out a hand, the warmth of her skin a stark contrast to the coolness of the forest air. Relief washed over me when I felt the steady rhythm of her pulse beneath my touch.

I looked down at the woman whose life I had saved, and the questions that had been swirling in my mind finally surfaced. Who was she? What had led her to this remote corner of the forest, far from the safety of civilization? How did she walk directly into my trap?

Surely, it was impossible for me to leave her all alone; anything could get to her, and if I could help it, I wouldn't allow another life to be lost under my watch. The plan was simple: get her back to my place and wait till she awakened; then we could think about how to proceed.

I leaned down to carry her and noted how little she weighed; despite her unconscious state, her body twisted and thrashed against my touch as I held her against my chest. It was as if she was fighting against me.

Her unconscious form seemed to recoil as I began to walk, her limbs flailing. At that moment, I felt a pang of guilt wash over me, knowing that my attempts to help her were only adding to her suffering.

I gathered her fragile form securely into my arms, heedless of her instinctual struggles. With each step nearer to my cabin, I knew she was closer to comfort.

By the time I reached my cabin, a sense of unease settled over me like a heavy blanket. She had gotten worse; her breathing had grown shallow and erratic, her skin hot to the touch as fever ravaged her fragile form.

I placed her gently on the bed, and she immediately began to toss and turn fitfully, obviously getting lost in the grip of delirium. I watched helplessly as she writhed in agony, her body contorting with each wave of pain that crashed over her.

The immediate solution was undressing her, wiping her down, and lowering her fever, but I hesitated to invade her privacy that way. The thought made my stomach churn with a mixture of apprehension and guilt, but I pushed aside my own discomfort in favor of saving her life.

I'm sure modesty wouldn't be an issue since she was close to boiling to death. I tried to avert my gaze as I began to peel her dirty sweater off. She was dressed too warmly for the weather of the summer, and she was soaked through with sweat.

Pulling the sweater over her head and then the shirt, I inhaled sharply. The see-through bra she wore didn't do much for modesty in the least, and a large bruise marred the porcelain skin over her back and shoulder. She must have fallen hard.

That was probably why she stepped on the trap.

I set to work pulling the jeans down to her legs, and I knew I would have to cut them to allow her injured leg to pass. As I rolled the material down her thighs, my eyes were drawn to the curls clearly outlined against her matching underwear.

I would have loved to peel the silk down her legs, then unhook her bra, leaving her completely naked beneath my gaze, but the guilt wouldn't allow me. The sight of her exposed skin, vulnerable and unguarded, stirred something primal within me—a hunger that I hadn't known existed.

I didn't think it was possible that I could get any harder just by watching. Every nerve ending in my body was on full alert, and I couldn't help but feel a surge of unexpected desire coursing through me.

But I forced myself to focus, pushing aside the unfamiliar sensations that threatened to consume me. She was injured, feverish, and unconscious, and all I could think about was having a better look at her perfect body.

With great care and practiced efficiency, I lowered her feverish body into a cool bath, the water soothing her overheated skin as she slipped into a restless slumber.

Hours passed in a blur as I tended to her, my mind a whirlwind of conflicting emotions as I hoped and waited for her to wake. It was almost dawn when she finally stirred, her eyes fluttering open.

Beautiful ice-blue eyes stared at me in shock, confusion, and disorientation. Then, they showed fear when she noticed she wasn't dressed, and I was near her injured leg, replacing her bandage.

I braced myself for her reaction as she looked around wildly and then tried to scramble to her feet, only to stop in pain. I wasn't sure what reaction I expected, but nothing could have prepared me for the force of her slap; she reared back and hit me without holding back.

I realized that for a small woman like her, she packed quite a punch; the sharp sting erupted across my skin, sending a jolt of pain reverberating throughout my entire body. My head snapped to the side, the force of the slap knocking me off balance for a moment. For an instant, the world seemed to spin around me, a dizzying whirlwind of confusion and disbelief.

My hand instinctively rose to cradle the throbbing ache blooming on my cheek. The impact had been more than just physical—it had been a shock to my system, a sudden and unexpected assault on my senses.

But as the initial shock began to fade, a wave of indignation washed over me and my jaw clenched tight with a stubborn resolve. I straightened my posture, meeting her gaze and trying to remain calm.

I knew that her reaction was understandable. In her eyes, I was nothing more than a stranger—an intruder in her most vulnerable moment. Still, it didn't justify her slapping me for no reason.

"What the fuck was that for?" My voice was low and controlled, but I didn't miss her flinch.

"I should be asking you. Why are you in between my legs?"

2

ELENA

I can't die; I refuse to give up like this. Not without realizing my dreams and proving those snotty women wrong.

The first thing I became aware of as I slowly regained consciousness was the soothing coolness that enveloped me. It was a welcome relief from the oppressive heat and burning sensation that had plagued me for what seemed like an eternity.

For a brief, disoriented moment, I wondered if I had died and gone to hell, but from the temperature, I surmised that it had to be heaven. Hell wouldn't feel so good. I needed to see what heaven looked like for myself.

Blinking against the soft light filtering through my eyelids, I opened my eyes tentatively, fully expecting to be met with celestial vistas or fiery infernos. Instead, what greeted me was a somewhat rustic, homely cabin bathed in candlelight that seemed to emanate from every surface.

The pain in my legs distracted me, and I looked down to find out why it hurt so much. Then I saw him, right between my legs;

even from his crouched position, I could tell he was a large man. He exuded an aura of quiet strength and confidence. If this was indeed heaven, then he must be my guardian.

My gaze lingered on him, and I couldn't help but notice the undeniable allure of his presence. I felt the pain from the leg once more, and it successfully brought me back to earth; then it hit me—I was naked, except for the matching bra and underwear I wore that morning as an afterthought.

He raised his head slightly, and I noted how stunning he was; his expression looked like he was in pain yet he was strangely comforting. He moved around a little to get comfortable and spread his weight; a flush of embarrassment crept over me as I realized the intimacy of the moment.

I was naked without knowing why, and he was showing no sign of discomfort; neither did he seem to care about my modesty in the least. For a second, I was torn between the urge to hide myself away and the inexplicable desire to bask in his presence, to lay there for longer and revel in the moment.

I shut my eyes, trying not to believe the moment was actually happening. I remained that way for a moment or two; when I opened my eyes again, he was staring at me, his gaze steady and unwavering as he regarded me with a mixture of concern and curiosity.

The look in his eyes somehow spurred me into action; panic surged through my veins like wildfire, suddenly consuming all rational thought in its wake. Who was he? Why was he positioned in between my legs? Why was he touching me? How did he find me?

My heart hammered against my ribs with a frenzied intensity that threatened to suffocate me, and in that moment of raw terror, instinct took over, propelling me to action before I could fully comprehend the consequences.

The blinding pain in my leg couldn't stop me as I lashed out with full force, my hand connecting in a resounding slap that echoed through the room. The sound of flesh meeting flesh reverberated in the air as the sting of the impact sent shockwaves coursing through my own hand.

I felt a surge of adrenaline coursing through my veins, fueling my defiance and propelling me forward.

The man recoiled from the force of my blow; a look of shock and confusion flickered across his features. His eyes widened with disbelief at my sudden outburst. His expression darkened as he slowly raised a hand to his cheek.

Looking at him now, he no longer seemed like a guardian angel but a sinister figure cloaked in shadows, his intentions shrouded in darkness.

"What the fuck was that for?" His deep voice sent a shiver through me; I knew if he retaliated, I probably wouldn't survive it.

I refused to be intimidated and raised my chin, "I should be asking you. Why are you between my legs?"

His expression lightened, and he looked at me calmly. "Listen, I understand you're disoriented, and you don't know where you are. But, never raise your hands at me again, understand?"

I caught myself before my mouth could fall open - that's it? He wasn't going to be mad that I hit him? He wasn't going to hurt me? He spoke in a deep and commanding voice that somewhat soothed my fears, and I found myself nodding.

"Alright."

My mind was settling down, and I could see him better. I hadn't been wrong about his aura of undeniable allure; he was the kind of man who would command respect and attention without trying in every room.

His dark hair was long, framing a ruggedly handsome face that seemed chiseled from stone. With shoulders broad enough to fill a doorway, he possessed a physicality that spoke of strength and power, leaving no doubt as to his capabilities.

As my gaze traveled down his imposing frame, I couldn't help but notice the way his tight jeans hugged his muscular thighs, accentuating the powerful contours of his legs. And when my eyes fell upon the scuffed combat boots peeking out from beneath his pant legs, a shiver of anticipation ran down my spine.

There was something undeniably magnetic about a man in combat boots, a rugged charm that spoke of untamed wilderness and unbridled passion. As I took in the sight before me, I felt a pang of desire stir deep within me, igniting a fire that threatened to consume my every thought.

Even as I marveled at his undeniable appeal, a voice of caution whispered in the back of my mind, warning me of the dangers that lurked beneath his rugged exterior. For all his physical prowess and undeniable charm, there was an air of mystery surrounding him, a sense that he held secrets hidden behind his steely gaze.

Yet, I found myself drawn to him like a moth to a flame, unable to resist the pull of his magnetic presence. Near him, I felt alive, electrified by the raw energy that crackled between us, and I knew that no matter what dangers lay ahead, I was powerless to resist the lure of the man before me; I felt my nipples hardened in reaction.

He must have mistaken my reaction to me being in pain or fearing him because he moved closer and lay a hand on my bare shoulder. "Hey, relax. I'm not going to hurt you."

His touch was searing; it made a rush of heat flood my cheeks, coloring them crimson with embarrassment. I could feel the intensity of his gaze like a scorching flame, tracing a searing path down my skin as his eyes roamed over my body.

"Where am I?" I crossed my arms over my chest, instinctively seeking some semblance of modesty as I drew up my knees as well, attempting to shield as much of my body as I could.

"In my cabin," he responded calmly. "Are you hurting anywhere?"

My legs, head, and *pussy*, I thought, but I remained silent and wrapped my arms tighter around my body, feeling exposed and vulnerable. "Where are my clothes?"

"I washed and hung them out to dry. I'll give you a shirt to put on until they finish drying."

Despite the warmth enveloping the room, a shiver ran down my spine and goosebumps erupted across my skin. My nipples tightened painfully when he got up and strolled away, my eyes following his perfect buttocks.

He handed me a shirt and pants when he returned. "I'll turn around for you to dress," he said. "When you're done, tell me so I can turn around."

"Th-thank you," I managed to say, feeling a mix of gratitude and awkwardness.

As soon as he turned away, I scrambled to yank on the shirt, struggling with the pain in my leg. It hung down to my knees, the sleeves engulfing my arms. I hastily rolled them up to regain some semblance of looking normal.

I tried to pull on the oversized sweatpants, but I couldn't because of my hurt legs. I knew they would probably slip back down, so I dropped them. Well, he had already seen me in a lot less, I reasoned. At least the shirt covered most of my body. Hopefully, my clothes would be dry soon.

"You can turn around," I whispered.

His eyes immediately roamed over me, and as soon as he turned, he said, "Well, you don't look too bad, and it will work."

I shivered, not from fear but from the unmistakable sex appeal in his voice. How could a complete stranger make me feel so safe? I licked my lips, my heart racing with a mix of uncertainty and intrigue.

I should have been afraid. I mean, here I was, practically naked in a stranger's cabin, wearing nothing but this oversized shirt and underwear. It was a situation that would send me, and most people, into a panic on a normal day. But strangely, I didn't feel threatened by him.

It's ridiculous, really. Most men terrified me, and for good reason. I'd had my fair share of bad experiences. So, why was I sitting here, staring at him with a strange mix of curiosity and something else I couldn't quite put my finger on? Why did it feel like there was a magnetic pull drawing me closer to him when every instinct should have been screaming at me to run?

I should have made a mad dash for the door, to escape from this stranger's cabin as fast as my legs could carry me. But instead, I found myself rooted to the spot, unable to tear my gaze away from him. It was like I was under some kind of spell, and he was the enchanter holding all the power.

I would have rather stripped him down until only his combat boots remained rather than run.

"Are you alright? You look a bit flushed." I swallowed and nodded; I was making a fool of myself. "Do you remember how you got here?" he asked.

I thought about his question for a moment, and then it all came rushing back. I remembered chasing the perfect shot, the adrenaline coursing through my veins as I captured the beauty of the wilderness with excitement.

I remembered losing my way after my compass broke when I stumbled over a fallen branch and went crashing to the ground; then I rolled over and felt the sharp pain in my right leg and my camera fell far out of my reach. I was trying to get it when blackness took over my vision.

Everything else faded into the background as a singular thought consumed my mind; I had to find my camera, no matter what.

"My camera." I was close to panicking; it was the most important thing I owned.

I was already reaching around blindly, trying to find something to help me stand up.

"I didn't spend hours stitching you up and tending to your pain so you could hurt yourself over some damn camera," he snapped. "How important is the camera anyway?"

"Don't you dare talk to me that way. Did I ask you to save me?" Maybe his looks were the only good trait he had. How could he make me angry so fast?

"Oh really? You would have wanted me to leave you out there to die?" he scoffed. "What a new way of saying thank you."

"Yes! If it meant I wouldn't have to grovel before you just because you saved me!" It was bad manners, but I couldn't let him continue talking badly about my beloved camera. He didn't know how important it was to me.

"What?" He looked at me in disbelief. "I can't believe this. Do you know it's nighttime already, and there's a heavy downpour on the way? Do you know how frightening the weather is this deep in the woods? So, you would risk all that and your hurt leg and your neck over the camera?"

"Yes! I don't care," I answered emphatically.

He looked like he wanted to say something mean, but he closed his eyes and paused for a moment. "Fine, would you at least let me help you?"

I almost sighed in relief; I thought he would never ask. There was no way I could manage on my injured leg.

"Fine." Then, knowing I sounded like a spoiled brat, I tried to do better. "I'm Elena."

He eyed me from the corners of his eyes. "Logan."

3

Logan

In the hour after she woke up, I learned a few important things about her. Her name was Elena, a beautiful name that suited her; she was gorgeous enough to take my breath away and make me ache in between my legs without relief in sight.

She was fiercely stubborn and probably used to getting her way with everything; she loved her camera more than her own life, and she wouldn't allow me to help her walk because of her pride. So she relied on a long stick and hobbled beside me.

She slowed down our walk as we went out in search of her camera; I knew it wouldn't be long before the storm came, and the torchlight that lit our way could only show a few feet ahead of us.

Twenty minutes later, we were deep in the forest but not remotely close to where she fell. She was slowing us down and it was already too late to turn back, not that she would accept that anyway. I was about to voice how foolish it was that we were risking our lives over some stupid camera, but it was too late.

The storm descended upon us with a fury I hadn't anticipated. Dark clouds loomed overhead, and the once tranquil forest was now a chaotic symphony of roaring winds and pounding rain. Elena stumbled at that same instance, her injured leg giving out beneath her. I resisted the urge to swear, but instead crouched next to her. I could see the blood.

"We need to find shelter," I shouted over the howling wind, my heart pounding with urgency. "We can't be caught in the storm."

For the first time since we began to walk, she looked as if she just realized how stupid it was to risk our necks; she nodded without a word, even as she grimaced in pain. *Serves her right*, I thought, but I sobered quickly.

I scanned the surroundings, searching for any semblance of refuge amidst the relentless downpour. And then I remembered the cave, hidden deep within the woods, a sanctuary from the elements that I had stumbled upon during one of my solitary hikes.

Gently, I lifted Elena into my arms, glad that she didn't try to resist; instead, she settled against my chest snugly. The rain stung my skin, and the wind threatened to knock us off balance as I navigated the treacherous terrain, but I pressed on, my focus solely on getting her to safety.

It was as if the very heavens had opened up, unleashing their wrath upon the unsuspecting earth below. Dark clouds moved overhead like malevolent giants, their ominous presence casting a pall over the once tranquil forest.

The air crackled with electricity, charged with the energy of the tempest brewing above. The wind howled like a banshee, whipping through the trees with a ferocity that seemed almost sentient. Every gust threatened to uproot us, to send us tumbling like leaves caught in a maelstrom.

We finally reached the mouth of the cave, and a sense of relief washed over me like a wave crashing upon the shore. I was glad I didn't miss it. The cave was a small alcove nestled amidst the rocks, offering scant protection from the storm, but it would cover us; the only problem was the chill in the air.

Carefully, I laid Elena down, my hands shaking slightly as I checked her injury. The intimacy of our sudden proximity and the vulnerability of our shared predicament seemed heightened by the raging tempest outside.

I peeled away the wet bandage, revealing the extent of the damage. With steady hands, I cleaned the wound, my touch gentle yet firm, my thoughts consumed with ensuring her well-being.

As I bandaged her leg again, our eyes met, and in that fleeting moment, she immediately looked away, not daring to complain about whatever pain she might be feeling; I didn't make mention of it, either.

The storm continued to rage outside and within the confines of the cave, tension simmered beneath the surface. The 'I told you so' remained unspoken, and I noted how she tried to make herself as small as possible.

"You know you can just yell if you're mad at me," she said after a while, obviously not willing to admit her fault just yet.

"I don't need to yell because I'm mad. Besides, I'm not mad at you," I replied. I was mad at myself for not trying harder to keep her in the cabin and from suffering uselessly now.

"Well, at least you can say 'I told you,' can't you?" It sounded as if her lips were chattering.

"You just said it, so I don't need to. Besides, the camera must be very important to you, right?" I wasn't sure why I was so fixated on making her feel better.

She didn't respond, and I looked back, flashing the torch I was holding in her direction to see her better. Her lips were blue, and her eyes were dilating as she shivered uncontrollably; fuck!

Her body probably couldn't handle the warmth from fever for a few hours and being drenched in the cold rain afterward.

"Damn! You could have said you were cold," anger laced my voice as worry tightened my throat.

It was useless to offer her my clothes since they were wet too, and I couldn't possibly tell her to remove the shirt she had on over the sexy matching underwear; I thought of a solution she might not like, but it was necessary.

"Fuck, come here." I opened my arms. "We need to share our body warmth."

I expected her to balk at the suggestion and maybe think I was trying to take advantage of her, but she did neither. Instead, she turned around, gingerly placing her injured leg aside as she snuggled against me.

I immediately held her close, feeling her weight against me and the thundering of her heart. I started to rub her arms for warmth, but the sensation of Elena's body pressed against mine sent a jolt of electricity through me, igniting a spark of attraction that I couldn't ignore.

Caught off guard by the intensity of my need, I struggled to contain the surge of desire coursing through my veins as I hardened. Every brush of her skin against mine sent waves of heat radiating through me, awakening a hunger that I'd long tried to suppress.

It was even more embarrassing since I knew she could feel my reaction against her backside as she was seated on my lap. Her lips fell open in a slight gasp, and I heard her sharp intake of breath as she shifted.

"Don't do that," I groaned; it was enough punishment to have the vivid image of her body in my head and her soft ass pressed against me.

"Can I do this then?" she asked and leaned forward, catching me off guard.

Our lips met in a heated kiss, and it was as if the world around us faded away, leaving only the two of us in our intimate cocoon.

She tasted of rain and just a hint of sweetness; she was the first course I'd long looked forward to, and I was damn certain I wouldn't stop with just sampling. I took control of the kiss, deepening it as she opened up with a moan, welcoming me inside as her hands splayed into my hair to hold my head.

This was what I'd longed to do since the moment I set my eyes on her; it had been forever since I felt this pull toward a woman and allowed myself to explore it. I wasn't sure I would be able to resist her; it was strong enough to make me forget all my vows about keeping people at arm's length to protect them from my curse.

"I want you so bad," I panted against her lips as I came up for air. "If I kiss you again, there's no stopping."

"I... I don't know what to do." It wasn't a refusal

"Just go with it, Elena. Trust me," I reassured her.

She nodded, and I immediately slid off her shirt with far less ceremony. I looked down at her body hungrily. I might have felt self-conscious in front of her perfect body, with her narrow hips and the tight muscles of her smooth stomach and chest, if I wasn't well-built.

The only light was from the torch that lay abandoned in the corner, and it felt so right to be with her there. I kissed her, feeling the whole length of her body against mine as I reached to unhook her bra.

Her breasts spilled free; they were beautiful like I had imagined and ample enough to fill my hands and swell over them.

Her nipples were dusty pink, and they stood proudly. She was perfect. I wanted to ravage them wildly, but I reminded myself that we were just getting to know each other's bodies.

Slowly, I raised her up and used my teeth to pull her panties down before settling her against the smooth side of the cave. When I settled between her thighs, she gasped and squeezed her eyes shut, giving herself over to the pleasure that coursed through her like a ravaging flame.

"This is what I've been fantasizing about," I murmured as I gazed at her. She sank against the cave, letting out a moan as the soft, wet heat of my mouth met her with such intimacy that all she could do was close her eyes and let me transport her.

I started slowly and then moved faster, using my tongue to unfold her until I found her small, round prize. She trembled and clenched her thighs tighter around my head, urging me on as I found her clitoris.

I circled my tongue around it with a growing intensity that made her grasp at my hair, twisting the strands in her hand. Her legs bent, her toes curled, and when she tried to pull my head up to make me stop before I went too far, I flashed her a wicked grin and pulled her legs apart, spreading her open.

She lay there, splayed out to me unashamedly. I loved that. I slipped my tongue down to lick deep inside her, the wetness smearing across my lips and down my chin. Then I found her clitoris again, swirling in circles harder and harder until her entire body was concentrated in that one bundle of nerves.

When she clawed at my shoulder, I knew she was close. Her orgasm pulsed through her, and she screamed it out, making me harder in my pants. I was so swollen that I knew there would probably be an imprint of my zipper against my dick.

I waited for her to come down from her high before I finally pulled the nipple that had been calling out to me in my lips. Suckling gently at first, then applying more pressure when she began to writhe, I realized I was getting harder from her pleasure.

It made me hope she would be ready for what was coming when I began to take my own pleasure. I would be selfish about it, and it was why I put her pleasure first; I slid a finger, then two, inside her to prepare her for my size.

She leaned back and rocked against my fingers, deriving her pleasure, and I knew she was ready. I was inside her in one sharp thrust, and she cried out; I paused, knowing she probably needed time to adjust to my size.

I remained still with difficulty until she gave me permission, opening her legs wider so I could sink in deeper, tracing a finger over my nipples and biting my earlobe. I started to move within her, pulsing rhythmically and steadily.

My hands found her breasts, and I held them, massaging them as I sucked on her left nipple, rolling and pinching her nipple between my forefinger and thumb as I buried my face in her hair, biting her shoulder, moving in and out until her cries filled the night.

When she came again, unable to hold back another second, I maintained the same quick strokes that had brought her to climax and then fell forward, my palms on the rock, my mouth still sucking at her nipple as I pulled it with me as far as it would go.

I finished with long, deep thrusts and then collapsed on top of her, releasing her nipple and finally brushing her hair away from her face. I remained inside her, wanting to feel every last bit of the moment.

4

ELENA

I wasn't sure whether it took minutes or hours, but I was certain it took a while before my breathing eventually evened out. As my heart and pulse slowed, my body quieted, and I began to reason things clearly. I found myself lying against a part of the cave that was smooth and had warmed up with our combined body heat.

I realized that I loved his weight on me; it made me feel safe despite the storm that continued to rage outside. I could feel his hand gently caressing my hair and supporting my weight with the other arm.

The clarity of what I'd done and what just took place dawned, and I felt the first stirring of embarrassment, unease, and shame.

What the heck had just happened? Never before had my need for sex been so...intense. Never, not even when I was ovulating, had I been so wildly out of control and lost all form of rational thought.

And never, ever, had I continued to feel such intense need blossoming for a man when I was still weak and trembling from my last release. Yet my sore pussy continued to pulsate, hot, heavy, and aching.

Despite a harsh inner voice that kept insisting I'd made a huge mistake by having sex with him in the first place, I felt an overwhelming urge for him to continue where he stopped; I tamped the need to take him in my mouth and give him as much pleasure as he had given me.

To taste the dick inside my mouth and guide him inside me for the second time so I could find out if the next orgasm would be as mind-blowing as the last two had been.

But I didn't. Instead, I squeezed my eyes shut and forced myself to lie still, not to react, respond, or allow my pussy to drip wetness, even as he began to massage my sore shoulder with his fingertips, and a fresh rush of need moved through me.

Thankfully, after a few minutes, his fingers stilled.

"Lena? Are you okay?" Fuck, everyone called me Elena; but Lena from his lips had me tightening my core from the sudden bolt of arousal that flashed through me.

I was definitely not okay; I was far from it. I needed some time and space to put what had just happened into perspective. I needed to think and figure out how best to explain that this was my first experience of this kind.

It wasn't every day that I saw a handsome stranger and jumped into their arms. I needed...

Stop it, Elena, the little voice in my head said in annoyance. *You wanted nothing more than for him to fuck you senselessly since the moment you set your eyes on him. Now, you have to live with the consequences and stop trying to justify your actions.*

I took a deep breath, recognizing the truth when I heard it. Just as I admitted to myself that no matter how much this was out of character, I would probably still do the same thing if he tried to touch me again; I just had to learn to live with it.

"Lena?" he said again, starting to sound worried, and I knew the nickname wasn't a mistake the first time.

I consciously tamped down my thoughts and pushed slightly against him to detangle our bodies. He immediately rolled to one side, braced himself on one elbow, and looked down at me.

"I'm fine, Logan. Why?"

He stared at me, his eyes concerned as they roamed over my face. "Because for a woman who just orgasmed after sex, you seem a little tense and withdrawn." He shrugged. "Well, I might be wrong, but that's what I feel."

"Oh," I replied, trying to get over how attuned he was.

"So, what's the matter?" He persisted.

I sighed and tried to play it cool. "I'm sorry you feel that way. It's just that everything happened too fast, and I'm just trying to put everything in perspective."

His expression changed, going from concerned to terrified in a second. "Fuck, did I hurt you? I knew I should have slowed down and been gentler. I guess I lost control for a minute there."

His words warmed my heart; it felt good to know I wasn't the only one who felt off-kilter. "No, you didn't hurt me. Trust me. It was amazing, more than amazing."

A look came over his face, a sort of shy amazement I'd never seen on a man before. "It felt great for me, too; I didn't know it could be like that."

Awkwardness settled over me again like a heavy blanket, weighing down my thoughts and making my heart race with uncertainty, but I noted with some surprise that I didn't move to cover up.

It was my first time in this situation, and I felt content to lay there as his hands trailed over my body, basking in the rush of sensations that tingled throughout, even if I couldn't shake the feeling of vulnerability that lingered in the air between us.

We fell silent, and I lay there, trying to rid myself of what was left of the negative emotions. I realized that I didn't even know him—not really. Sure, we'd shared a moment of intimacy, but it was fleeting, and now we were left with the aftermath, unsure of what to say or how to act.

I watched him, and I couldn't help but feel a curiosity bubbling within me. Who was this man who had just shared such an intimate moment with me? What were his hopes, his fears, his dreams?

I knew I couldn't speak for him, but perhaps it wouldn't hurt to try to get to know him a little better. After all, he had taken care of me, protected me from the storm, and saved my sorry ass.

There was also a kindness in his eyes, a tenderness in his touch that made me wonder if there was more to him than met the eye.

The storm continued to rage outside. The cave provided a temporary sanctuary from the relentless wind and rain, and we had nothing else to do, so I wanted to start getting to know him.

"I didn't get around to thanking you for saving me," I began gently, "I don't know what I would have done all alone in the storm with an injured leg."

He didn't say a word; he simply squeezed my shoulder. First things first, I noted that he was probably a man of few words.

"Why are you out here all alone?" I asked, my voice echoing softly in the confined space of the cave. "You know your way around and even have a cabin here. Don't you get scared?"

Logan turned to look at me, his eyes dark and intense in the dim light. There was a flicker of something in his expression, a hint of wariness that made me wonder what he was hiding.

"I guess you could say I'm used to it," he replied cryptically, his voice low and guarded. "I spent a lot of time alone before I left the military. It's just easier for me since I like being alone."

Okay, I'd learned three more things about him: he liked to keep secrets, he was alone, and he was formerly in the military.

His words sent a shiver down my spine, and I couldn't help but feel a sense of unease settle over me. There was something about the way he spoke, something elusive and secretive that made me suspect he wasn't telling me the whole truth.

But I didn't press him further. Instead, I remained silent, unwilling to push him to reveal more than he wanted.

"And what about you?" Logan's gaze was piercing as he turned his attention back to me. "What made you venture out into the wilderness alone? That's dangerous for anyone not to mention a woman of your size."

I hesitated, unsure of how much to reveal. The memory of what had driven me to flee from home still lingered fresh in my mind. "I needed to get away," I admitted finally, "My normal routine was suffocating me, and I needed some space to clear my head."

I cleared my throat before continuing, "But being here wasn't planned at all. My compass got damaged, and I lost my way while taking pictures with my camera. Then I fell and rolled into the trap and lost the camera in the process."

Logan studied me intently, his eyes probing and searching as if trying to uncover the truth hidden beneath my words. "Sure, I can understand that," he said quietly. "Sometimes, it's nice to escape from it all and just be alone with your thoughts."

I nodded in agreement, but inside, I was grateful that he didn't press. But there was something about his demeanor, something that didn't quite add up. It was as if he was holding something back, something important that he wasn't ready to share.

I shook my head; it wasn't my place to judge or nag since I wasn't being totally honest either.

"But it can also be lonely," I added as an afterthought.

Logan's gaze softened. "I know what you mean," he said softly. "But sometimes, solitude is better than other options."

There was nothing more I could say; we settled into a tense silence, each lost in our own thoughts as the wind and storm continued to howl outside. It took about another hour of heavy downpour before it finally slowed to a drizzle and then a stop.

"It's too late to look for your camera; it's already midnight. I'll check for it tomorrow; let's head back."

After seeing what happened because of my stubbornness, there was no way I could argue against that, so I nodded and allowed him to help me dress.

The air was cool and crisp as we emerged from the cave, the lingering scent of rain mixing with the earthy aroma of the forest. Each breath felt like a cleansing of the soul.

The path back to his cabin was familiar, yet somehow different in the darkness of the night. The trees swayed gently in the breeze, their leaves whispering secrets of resilience and renewal.

I hobbled after him silently, gritting my teeth against the onslaught of pain in my leg, I shouldn't have refused his help earlier, and my pride wouldn't allow me to ask.

When the cabin appeared ahead, nestled among the trees like a sanctuary of warmth and safety, I breathed a sigh of relief, looking forward to getting off my feet. Even with the limited light, I couldn't help but marvel at the simple beauty of the structure, its weathered wood blending seamlessly with the forest landscape.

Inside, the air was warm and inviting, infused with the comforting scent of wood smoke and homemade soup. Logan moved with purpose, his movements fluid and sure as he tended to the fire and warmed the soup.

I watched him with a sense of awe, struck by the quiet strength and resilience that seemed to emanate from him like a force of nature. His demeanor shifted seamlessly from a guide to a caretaker.

He wasted no time tending to the wound on my leg; his touch was gentle and sure, and he cleaned and bandaged it with practiced efficiency while the soup warmed. Each brush of his fingers against my skin sent a shiver of awareness coursing through me, igniting a fire that had been smoldering between us since the moment we met.

The warmth of the fire cast dancing shadows across the cabin, enveloping us in a cocoon of intimacy as Logan worked. I couldn't tear my eyes away from him, captivated by the strength and tenderness in his movements.

There was something undeniably magnetic about the way he cared for me as if each touch was infused with a silent promise of protection and devotion. He finished tending to my leg, and our eyes met; at that point, I saw a flicker of something raw and primal in his gaze—a hunger that mirrored my own.

"Fuck, why are you looking at me like that?'" he growled as he closed the distance between us, his presence filling the space between our bodies with an electric charge.

His lips captured mine in a searing kiss that left me breathless and wanting more. At that moment, all the barriers between us seemed to melt away, leaving nothing but the heat of our passion and the longing that pulsed between us like a heartbeat.

I closed my eyes in delight and allowed him to carry me to the bed and please me; he seemed to derive his pleasure from mine. When I felt his long and thick dick probing at the puffy, juicy lips to bury himself in my burning pussy, I was ready.

His dick was cold as he slid inside me; it drove me insane. Everywhere he touched, he left tiny shocks of pleasure in his wake. I shuddered as he found my clit and rubbed it, pushing me toward the edge of ecstasy.

I felt my orgasm building, and every suck, every lick, every touch from him drove me closer to the fall. My knuckles strained white as I held onto the edge of the bed. The room spun around me in ecstasy, and I was ready to fall.

I pumped my hips against his sinful pleasuring. I fucked his dick wildly, urging him on. I held onto the bed frame harder and felt as if I were going to pass out from sheer pleasure.

I thrust my hips forward and screamed at the top of my lungs as I came, grateful no one else could hear us. The steady thrust into my sore pussy and against my sensitive clit drove my orgasm higher and higher. I couldn't stop screaming at the intensity of my orgasm.

The pleasure blinded me, and my entire body shook violently. He continued to thrust until he finished with a groan, still buried deep inside of me. My body shook sporadically as I came down from my blissful high.

The cabin slowly stopped whirling out of focus around me while I sagged helplessly on the bed. I had never experienced an orgasm as powerful as the one I'd just had.

The entire insides of my legs, from my still dripping pussy to my weak, limp ankles, were coated with a slick sheen of my juices. Boy, he was good, and it would have been a shame to miss out on that.

But that didn't mean we could continue.

5

Logan

I knew even before the nightmare started.

As usual, the darkness crept in like a malevolent fog, thick and suffocating, swallowing me whole and dragging me back into the depths of my own personal hell. It was as if time itself had folded back on me, and suddenly, I was back on the front lines, surrounded by the chaos and carnage of war.

The air was thick with the acrid stench of smoke and death, choking me with its bitter embrace. Gunfire crackled in the distance, a relentless symphony of destruction that pounded against my eardrums like a drumbeat of doom. Each explosion sent shockwaves through my body, rattling my bones and leaving me trembling in their wake.

I could feel the weight of my gear pressing down on me, the straps digging into my shoulders like a constant reminder of the burden I carried. My boots sunk into the muck with each step, the ground slick with blood and mud, threatening to swallow me whole with every move I made.

But it was the faces that haunted me the most—the faces of my fallen comrades, their eyes wide with terror and pain, their mouths open in silent screams of agony. I reached out to them, desperate to offer some semblance of comfort in their final moments, but they slipped through my fingers like smoke, leaving me grasping at shadows.

And then it happened—the bomb blast tore through the air with a deafening roar, ripping apart everything in its path with merciless precision. I was thrown to the ground, my body twisting and contorting in ways it was never meant to, as flames licked at my skin and shrapnel tore through the air like deadly rain.

In the aftermath, there was only silence—a heavy, suffocating silence that hung in the air like a shroud. I was left alone amidst the wreckage, the sole survivor in a sea of devastation, haunted by the ghosts of those I couldn't save.

I awakened with a start, my heart pounding in my chest and sweat slicking my skin. The nightmare was over, but the memories lingered, etched into my mind like scars that will never fade.

I lay there in the darkness, and I knew that sleep would elude me once again, leaving me to wrestle with the demons that lurked within the darkest corners of my soul. I tried to remain quiet as I got up and made my way outside.

I didn't want to disturb Elena, who seemed to be sleeping well for the first time in days; she was the other thing that had been plaguing my mind other than my dreams. She had changed over the past few days, and since our sex on the day she arrived, she seemed withdrawn and content to be alone.

If there was something I was certain of, it was the fact that trouble was brewing anytime a woman was silent and standoffish. It was a lesson I'd learned while in the army, through countless encounters with women who wore their emotions like armor, keeping their true feelings hidden behind a facade of indifference.

I watched her from across the room as she slept; I couldn't help but notice the tightness in her shoulders. Even when she was awake, I never missed the way she avoided meeting my gaze and the subtle tension in her jawline. It was clear that something was bothering her, something she wasn't ready—or willing—to share with me.

I tried to ignore the nagging sense of unease that settled in the pit of my stomach, but it was impossible to shake the feeling that I was walking into a minefield, each step fraught with the risk of triggering an explosion.

I stopped asking since the other day; the conversation replayed in my head, thankfully drowning out the lingering thought from the nightmare.

"What's on your mind?" I asked, unable to bear the silence any longer. Her response was a noncommittal shrug, her eyes fixed on some distant point beyond the confines of the cabin.

I felt the frustration bubbling up inside me, frustration at her unwillingness to open up, to let me in. But beneath the frustration was a deeper, more primal emotion—a gnawing fear that whatever was troubling her would drive a wedge between us, but I couldn't very well force her to talk.

I tried reaching out to her, my hand hovering uncertainly in the space between us, unsure if she would welcome the gesture or recoil from my touch. To my surprise, she didn't pull away, allowing me to gently brush a stray lock of hair behind her ear.

"Talk to me," I urged, my voice soft with concern. "Are you hurting somewhere?"

For a moment, she seemed to waver as if unsure if she should take the leap into the unknown. And then, with a sigh that seemed to carry the weight of the world, she finally spoke.

"It's nothing," she said, but the lie was clear as day.

I wanted to press her further, to demand that she tell me what was really going on, but I held my tongue, knowing that pushing her would only drive her further away. Instead, I let her be.

As the days passed, I grew more uneasy with Elena's silence. It wasn't just her quietness that troubled me, but the subtle shifts in her demeanor, the way her laughter lost its sparkle, and her smiles seemed forced. It was as if a shadow had fallen over her, dimming the light that usually radiated from her vibrant spirit.

Every time I glanced in her direction, I found myself searching her face for any sign of what might be troubling her, but she was a master at masking her emotions, her expressions guarded and inscrutable. It was like trying to decipher a cryptic code, each glance revealing a new layer of complexity that only deepened the mystery.

I longed to reach out to her, to wrap her in my arms and chase away whatever demons haunted her thoughts, but I didn't, afraid of overstepping the boundaries. I knew from experience that sometimes the wounds we carried were too raw to be shared, too painful to be exposed to the light of day.

So instead, I tried to occupy myself with the mundane tasks of everyday life, throwing myself into my hunting and preparing for winter with a fervor born of desperation. But no matter how busy I kept myself, thoughts of her weighed heavily on my mind, a constant presence that refused to be ignored.

In the quiet moments between tasks, my thoughts always, invariably drifted back to her, searching for clues that might unravel the mystery of her silence. But each time, I came up empty-handed, left with nothing but a sense of frustration and helplessness that gnawed at my insides like a hungry beast.

As the days turned into a week, the tension between us grew palpable, a thick fog that obscured the path forward. I knew that something had to give, that we couldn't continue like this forever, but I also knew that forcing the issue would only drive her further away.

I decided that my waiting around was done, and the other thing I knew about women was the fact that most couldn't resist romantic gestures. Maybe that would finally give me a breakthrough.

I looked outside at the dark and gloomy sky; there would probably be no sun, and it was as perfect as any day to have a romantic time. Later, I would come to wonder why she was affecting me so much and why I was more fixated on making her happy rather than wishing for her to leave as soon as possible.

After all, I went so deep into the forest so I could be alone. But the thought didn't occur.

Setting the scene took more effort than I had anticipated, but I was determined to make it special for Elena. As she slept soundly in the other room, I tiptoed around the cabin, careful not to disturb her; I prepared our makeshift candlelit dinner.

I lit the candles one by one, their flickering flames casting a warm glow over the room, and set the table with care, arranging the plates and cutlery just so. I wished I had some soft strains of music filling the air, adding to the ambiance, but I would have to make do with what I had.

I moved around the kitchen, preparing a simple yet elegant meal; the scent of sizzling herbs and spices filled the air, mingling with the aroma of freshly caught meat roasting over an open flame.

First, I carefully seasoned the meat with a blend of wild herbs I had foraged from the forest, infusing it with flavors of rosemary, thyme, and sage. Then, I wrapped the filets in banana leaves, sealing in the moisture and allowing the flavors to meld together as they cooked.

Next, I turned my attention to the side dishes, rummaging through the meager supplies to find ingredients to complement the main course. With a handful of wild mushrooms and some tender greens I had gathered the day before, I whipped up a simple salad dressed with a tangy vinaigrette made from foraged berries and a splash of vinegar.

For a starchy accompaniment, I improvised a rustic potato dish, slicing the tubers thinly and layering them with onions and garlic before baking them in a cast-iron skillet until golden brown and crispy on the edges.

I couldn't resist indulging in a sweet treat to end our meal on a high note. With a handful of ripe berries I had picked from the bushes near the cabin, I whipped up a simple fruit compote, simmering the berries with a splash of honey and a sprinkle of cinnamon until they were soft and syrupy.

I plated each dish with care, arranging them artfully on the table; I couldn't help but feel a swell of pride at what I had accomplished with so little.

Finally, everything was ready, and I took a moment to admire my handiwork before going to wake Elena. As I gently shook her awake, I could see the confusion in her eyes, quickly replaced by the indifference she had perfected over the past few days.

I didn't allow it to get to me, "You must be hungry; I made food."

I could see denial spring to her lips, but she swallowed it down when her stomach grumbled loudly. Knowing her leg was still too tender to walk on, I leaned down and swooped her in my arms, thankful when she didn't complain.

I walked into the candlelit room with Elena in my arms; my heart warmed up when her eyes widened in surprise at the sight before her. The rustic charm of the cabin's interior was accentuated by the flickering light of the candles, casting dancing shadows on the wooden walls.

Her delight was palpable as she took in the cozy ambiance, a soft smile playing on her lips as she turned to me. "Logan, this is... incredible. When did you prepare all this?"

I couldn't help but return her smile. "Not too long ago. It didn't take long," I lied.

As we settled at the table, the scents of the freshly cooked meal wafted through the air. Elena's eyes met mine, and for a moment, it felt as though time stood still before she tore her gaze away and sampled the meat.

"A handsome man who can cook." She moaned as she closed her eyes and chewed. "Marry me already," she joked, but her words stabbed me in the heart.

"I'm glad you like it," I commented before delving in.

We were halfway through the meal when she set her cutlery down and looked at me. "Let me guess."

"What?" I asked, not following what she meant.

"You did all of this because of my recent behavior?" She looked shy.

I wanted to deny it, but there was no need to do so. "I didn't know I was so easy to read."

"I would like to apologize for my recent behavior. But I was scared and ashamed of myself."

My eyebrows furrowed. What did she have to be scared and ashamed of?

She continued. "I was afraid you would think I was being easy. I mean, we are practically strangers, and I've only been here for a week and on the first day... well, we've already..." She trailed off, but I understood her perfectly; it became clear what she meant.

"You might not believe it, but I don't go around sleeping with every man I meet."

I reached across the table, gently squeezing her hand in reassurance. "Elena, what happened between us was... special. It wasn't about being easy or rushing into anything. Every moment was meaningful."

Her eyes widened, and she looked at me with emotions in her eyes, but she said nothing.

I couldn't help but feel a pang of guilt wash over me. Her worries mirrored my own fears, and I realized just how much we both had been holding back, afraid of misinterpreting each other's intentions.

"Elena, I want you to know that I would never want you to feel pressured or uncomfortable around me. I'm not sure if you would believe that I've been worried you were distant because you thought I might be taking advantage of you."

I reached across the table, gently brushing a stray lock of hair from her face. "Yes, I've only known you for a week, but you've come to mean a lot to me, Elena."

Her eyes softened at my words, a smile playing at the corners of her lips. "I believe you, Logan."

Feeling a weight lift off my shoulders, I suggested, "How about we take this opportunity to get to know each other better? After all, you're still here, at least until your leg heals enough to walk, and I would love nothing more than to spend more time with you."

"I have a very good idea. How about we play twenty-games?" she suggested; she seemed to have transformed right in front of me.

"That's fine, anything you want."

Much later, late at night, we settled into bed. Sleeping together for the very first time on the same bed, the warmth of Elena's body next to mine enveloped me like a cocoon. Her head found its resting place on my chest, nestled against my heartbeat, and I wrapped my arms around her, enfolding her in a tender embrace.

The soft rustle of the sheets provided a soothing backdrop to the symphony of our breaths, a harmonious melody that echoed the tranquility of the night. I pressed a soft kiss to the crown of her head, savoring the sweetness of the moment as her hair cascaded like silk over my skin.

In the embrace, the weight of the day's worries melted away, replaced by a profound sense of peace and serenity. Our bodies molded together seamlessly, fitting like puzzle pieces meant to be united in this intimate dance of affection.

Bathed in the ethereal glow of the moonlight streaming through the window, I closed my eyes, allowing myself to be enveloped by the tranquility of the moment and slept.

For the first time in forever, there was no nightmare.

6

ELENA

The morning was perfect; I felt well-rested and more in tune with myself than I'd been all week. It might have been my imagination, but I could almost swear that the painkiller in my system worked better than it had all week.

Sunlight filtered into the cabin in soft, golden streams, casting warm, inviting pools of light on the rustic wooden floor. Dust motes danced lazily in the gentle beams, adding a sense of tranquility to the cozy interior.

Through the windows, the lush greenery of the surrounding wilderness was bathed in a soft glow, creating a picturesque tableau of nature's beauty. The sunlight illuminated the natural textures of the cabin's furnishings, highlighting the rich grains of the wood and the earthy tones of the fabrics.

Everything was perfect, except Logan.

Watching the sunrise was almost as relaxing as looking at Logan. I shifted my gaze to the regal lines of his profile as he bent over, buckling his combat shoes. Not that I was trying to find fault. I was smitten by him, and everything he did.

On a good note, I felt relieved that he didn't know what was going on inside me; I'd done a fine job this morning appearing slightly infatuated, as I should have been since we'd pretty much passed the stage of being friends.

Usually, I would be tense to find out why either of us wasn't interested in putting a label on things; with anyone else, I would have ensured that I knew where I stood before going all the way. I was long past an age when I found anything admirable or attractive about unrequited love.

I also had more than enough self-respect to believe I deserved more than just a casual affair and roll in the sack. But the bottom line was that it felt different with him, which was why I wasn't willing to let him retreat behind the wall he'd built for himself overnight, thanks to whatever it was that was bothering him so terribly.

Perhaps I was deluding myself into thinking he was as smitten as I was, but I believed it was because he did care for me, maybe more than he realized - surely more than he'd ever admit.

The evidence was there in the hunger of his lovemaking, the way he held me tight in his sleep, the way he tried hard to bring me out of my shell when I shut him out, the way he arranged the romantic meal, and how he had gone through thick and thin to find my camera.

Although it wasn't anything much, it was a start, something to build on. I smiled and put my errant thoughts out of my mind, determined not to push him too much. Maybe if I acted just fine, everything would work out.

"Are you going hunting?" I began, infusing cheeriness into my voice.

"Yeah. I need to check the traps and get more wood for winter." I wasn't sure why the thought of him preparing for winter in the wilderness made me sad and even more curious about why he chose to live there.

I got up and hobbled to where he was standing. "Do you want me to come along? I can be of help."

"No, it's fine. You're hurt. I will get things done faster." His words came out in a rush, and he looked almost panicked.

"I'm sure I can manage; I promise not to get in your way." I tried again.

"No!" His word came out sharply before he reached out to touch my shoulder; it was enough to tell that he didn't want me there.

Our eyes met, and just like that, awareness simmered between us. Looking into his handsome face, I was reminded of all the intimacies we'd recently shared. I could see from his shuttered expression that he was remembering, too.

I reached out and closed my hand around his. After a moment's hesitation, his fingers curled around mine. As if that was all the closeness he could handle, however, he looked back at the lake. "I'll be back before you know it."

He didn't wait for a reply before he strolled out, leaving me feeling rebuffed by his frosty response. It was such a letdown since I'd been feeling buoyed by the progress we'd made since the previous night's intimacy.

Maybe that's why the rejection landed like a punch to the gut, leaving me reeling. Just hours earlier, we had shared an electrifying connection, and now it felt like I was being shut out. Doubts crept in, taunting me with questions about what I might have done to trigger such a response.

Despite the ache of rejection, I fought to push aside my disappointment and grasp understanding. Maybe Logan needed some privacy disguised as hunting to clear his mind, or perhaps there were deeper reasons for his desire to be alone. Regardless, I resolved to respect his decision, though it left me feeling adrift in uncertainty.

I couldn't resist watching him walk away and didn't stop looking until he vanished into the dense foliage. Part of me yearned to go after him, to demand an explanation, but a quieter voice urged patience and restraint.

It whispered that giving him space was the kindest thing I could do, even if it left me feeling hollow and alone. I reminded myself gently that he did the same when I was in my feelings. But it also made me wonder if it was payback of some sort.

With a heavy sigh, I turned away, thinking of what to do. A walk in the woods would offer the clarity and peace of mind I so desperately craved, but I couldn't do much with my leg.

The morning light filtered through the curtains, casting soft shadows across the room as I returned to lay on the bed with its tangled sheets, making me remember how he had held me so close last night.

I couldn't shake the feeling that something was wrong, that some unseen specter haunted his mind and cast a shadow over our budding connection. His eyes, usually warm and inviting, held a distant look as if he were a million miles away.

I remained there for as long as I could, wondering if he would eventually open up to me and share his burden and if he felt the same way when I had shut him out. When my eyes fell on the camera he'd placed on the unpolished table, the urge to take pictures was irresistible.

It had been a miracle that the camera came out unscathed from my fall, and it survived the storm before Logan found it. He had cleaned it up with care and love; it looked as good as new.

My eyes fell on my leg, and I wondered how far it would take me, but I reasoned that I didn't have to go too far away before getting some good shots. The sun was filtering beautifully through the trees and casting long shadows across the forest floor when I finally dragged myself out.

Despite feeling unsettled by Logan's cold refusal, I left him a note so he wouldn't worry when he got back. The ache in my legs seemed to mirror the ache in my heart, and I knew I needed to find a way to distract myself.

The familiar weight of my camera kept me grounded in the present moment, and the twinge of pain with each step didn't allow me to get distracted as I ventured out into the wilderness surrounding the cabin.

The beauty of nature surrounded me, offering a welcome respite from the turmoil of my thoughts. I wandered along winding trails, my camera poised and ready to capture the wonders that lay hidden among the trees. With each click of the shutter, I felt a sense of release.

I'd almost forgotten how the act of photographing always allowed me to channel my emotions into something tangible and beautiful. I framed each shot, focusing on the intricate details of the world around me. My mind started to clear, replaced by a newfound sense of purpose and determination.

With each picture I took, I felt a sense of empowerment wash over me as if reclaiming control over my own narrative. It reminded me why I'd begun the journey, which led to me becoming lost and injured in the first place.

I'd been in search of a way to take back my power, and I was currently seeing it in the solace of the beauty that surrounded me.

I captured how high the sun was in the sky through the foliage and how its warm rays painted the landscape in hues of gold and amber. How the gentle breeze whispered through the trees, carrying with it the scent of pine and earth, a soothing balm to my restless spirit.

The beauty of nature unfolded before me in all its glory the more I walked, a breathtaking tapestry of color and light just waiting to be captured. I wandered through fields of wildflowers, their petals swaying gently in the breeze, and along winding forest paths, where shafts of sunlight filtered through the canopy above, casting dappled shadows on the forest floor.

I was free to explore and create, to find beauty in the most unexpected of places, and slowly, I began to lose track of time. With my camera in hand, I became a silent observer, a seeker of hidden treasures waiting to be unearthed. Each click of the shutter echoed through the silent woods, capturing moments of fleeting beauty that might otherwise have gone unnoticed.

I wondered what those rude and spoiled women would think if they could see me. The wonder made my mind drift back to the night of my first official gallery opening. I closed my eyes, and a whirlwind of emotions crashed against the shores of my consciousness.

I remembered how hard I worked to make things perfect, how the thrill of anticipation had coursed through my veins as I unveiled my collection to the world, my heart brimming with hope and pride.

The collections sold out fast, and it was not even halfway into the evening. So, I was feeling light and overjoyed until some of the women walked into the restroom and I overhead them.

I remembered the moment when I overheard their hushed conversations, the venomous words dripping with disdain and malice.

"Who does she think she is?" the first woman said.

"Did you see how she was strutting around feeling high and mighty without knowing why she's sold out?" the second woman backed her up.

I held my breath, needing to hear more. "Does she think we would be here if it weren't for her parents?" the third said.

"Hush, you're speaking too loudly. Remember, we have to be in their good graces so they can help us in the future," the first said again.

"Oh please, it's not as if her collection is to our taste or up to our standards. At least we can be honest between ourselves."

"Good for her; she is from an influential family. I'm so jealous," the second said as they filed out of the rest room.

Tears filled my eyes, but soon, a fire ignited within me, burning with a fierce determination to prove them wrong. I would have another opening under an alias. I left home a week later, leaving a note behind.

Lost in my thoughts and rhythm of photography, I barely noticed the shifting shadows and rustling leaves around me, my focus consumed by the breathtaking scenery that unfolded before my lens.

But then, as if summoned by some unseen force, a sense of unease prickled at the edges of my consciousness—a subtle shift in the air that set my nerves on edge.

My camera was still raised to my eye, so I instinctively sought out the source of my disquiet through its lens, and that's when I saw it—a massive boar, its form looming amidst the foliage like a specter of the forest.

I froze, my breath catching in my throat as I gazed at the creature through the narrow lens of my camera. A gasp escaped me as I lowered and faced the monstrous creature with my own eyes—a shrill, involuntary sound that echoed through the silent expanse of the forest.

The boar stood before me, its gaze steady and unwavering, as if assessing me with a mix of caution and curiosity. For a heartbeat, we remained locked in a silent standoff, each of us measuring the other with a wary gaze.

And then, with a flick of its massive head, a scream tore through me. My heart pounded against my ribs, each beat a thunderous echo in the stillness of the woods as I grappled with the primal fear that gripped me and I screamed again.

The scream tore through the tranquil silence of the forest like a jagged lightning bolt, its shrill notes slicing through the air with a primal urgency that sent shivers down my spine.

Every fiber of my being seemed to reverberate with the raw intensity of the sound. It was a primal instinct, an unbridled outcry of fear and desperation that reverberated through the dense foliage, echoing off the ancient trees like a haunting lament.

Was this how I was destined to die?

7

LOGAN

I must have thrown her off with my attitude. I could see the confusion on her face even though she hadn't said anything about it. I shook my head, thinking how irrational my behavior would seem to her.

Just the day before, I was doing all I could to reassure her and get her to break the walls she had around her. Yet, here I was, holding her at arm's length after holding her in my arms all night.

But I refused to feel guilty; instead, I continued strolling away from the cabin, needing to escape the sudden surge of emotions that were stirring within me. Hunting could honestly wait; we had enough supplies to last us for weeks, and I had been at it tirelessly for days.

No, what I needed was solitude, the quiet embrace of the forest that always seemed to offer solace. Sleeping for the first time and not having a nightmare was probably what threw me off; I knew I slept well because of her.

The memories of surviving that bomb blast, the chaos of battle and the weight of being the lone survivor had always been a part of my sleeping and waking moments. It was a nightmare that refused to release its grip, a constant reminder of the fragility of life and the horrors of war.

Holding Elena in my arms overnight had chased the darkness away and stirred up emotions that I had long buried, emotions that I needed to keep buried for my own sanity and her benefit.

I walked deeper into the woods, and the familiar sights and sounds of nature surrounded me, offering a comforting embrace. The rustle of leaves, the gentle sway of trees, the chorus of birdsong—all served as a soothing backdrop.

I found a secluded spot by a babbling brook and sank down onto a fallen log, letting the tranquility of the forest wash over me. Closing my eyes, I focused on the steady rhythm of my breaths, willing myself to find peace amidst the chaos of my thoughts.

The memory of surviving that bomb blast, the weight of being the lone survivor in the aftermath of an invasion came flooding back with a force that left me reeling.

It was a reminder of why I had chosen to remain in isolation in the first place, why I had built these walls around my heart to keep others out. She was just passing through, and I reminded myself that she was a temporary presence in my life.

She would be gone before I knew it, leaving me to return to the solitude I had grown accustomed to. Getting attached to her was the last thing I needed, a dangerous path that would only lead to heartache and disappointment.

I continued to sit by the brook and tried to push aside the emotions that threatened to consume me. I closed my eyes and focused on my breathing, willing myself to find the calm within the storm.

But try as I might, I couldn't shake the feeling of unease that lingered within me. Elena had a way of getting under my skin, of breaking through the barriers I had erected around myself. And though I knew it was foolish, I couldn't help but feel a twinge of longing for something, maybe, if the situation were different.

With a heavy sigh, I opened my eyes again and gazed out into the forest, into the dense canopy of trees. It was clear that I couldn't outrun my emotions, no matter how hard I tried. And as much as I wanted to deny it, there was a part of me that couldn't help but hope that maybe, just maybe, Elena would choose to stay.

But I know I couldn't do that to her; it would be unfair and selfish to hope for that. I couldn't expect her to give up everything and live the same way I was living.

The best thing I could do for her would be to keep my distance. Everyone who had ever been close to me had met a tragic end, from my mother to my dead ex-girlfriend. It seemed like a curse that followed me wherever I went, and I couldn't bear the thought of bringing that same fate upon Elena.

It would be best if she remained a beautiful stranger, a ray of light in the darkness of my solitude, and I didn't want to tarnish her brightness with the shadows of my past. It would be better for her if whatever connection had sparked between us remained a beautiful memory, untainted by the specter of death that haunted my every step.

The memories of those I had lost haunted me like ghosts in the darkness, their faces flickering in the shadows of my mind. My mother was taken too soon after my birth, my father was lost to cancer, and my ex-girlfriend died in a car accident; her tragic end still haunted my dreams.

Not to mention how my military peers died, and I survived alone and unscathed; there wasn't any other proof that I needed to know I was a curse to everyone around me. I condemned everyone who was meaningful to me to a fate of suffering and sorrow.

For Elena's sake, I would sacrifice my own happiness, content to watch from a distance as she moved on with her life, free from the shadow of death that followed me wherever I went.

That decided, the restless energy that had burned through me dissipated, leaving me exhausted. I knew I should probably go back to her and try to convince her to leave before her leg healed; I would be willing to risk going into town just for her sake. She deserved that much.

I turned to face the cabin, my thoughts finally slowing down, and I began to breathe more easily. I was getting closer to the cabin when her scream shattered the silence like a thunderclap, jolting me into action.

My blood froze, and my mind went into a frenzied panic. Without a second thought, I was dashing and running before I could even process what was happening. Her screams pierced the air, each one squeezing my heart as I imagined the danger she was in.

With each scream, my heart clenched tighter in my chest, driving me forward with an urgency I couldn't ignore. As I raced toward the source of her cries, the distance between us seemed to stretch endlessly, the expanse of the forest closing in around me like a suffocating blanket.

I burst into the clearing where her scream was coming from and skidded to a stop; my muscles tensed as I surveyed the scene, my mind racing to formulate a plan of action. She was holding her camera tightly and cowering in front of a boar.

The boar's snarls filled the air, a primal sound that sent shivers down my spine. Elena stood frozen in fear, her eyes locked on the beast as it circled closer, its tusks gleaming in the sunlight.

They typically didn't roam during the day, and I couldn't think why the boar was out and about.

Every instinct screamed at me to act, to protect her. With a surge of adrenaline, I launched myself forward, heedless of the danger that the boar represented. Branches whipped past me as I sprinted toward her, the ground uneven beneath my feet.

As I closed the distance between us, I could see the fear etched on Elena's face, her body trembling with every step the boar took. Time seemed to stretch and warp around us, the world reduced to a narrow tunnel of focus as I zeroed in on her safety.

With a primal roar of my own, I lunged toward Elena, wrapping my arms around her and pulling her away from the charging boar. The impact knocked us both off balance, sending us tumbling to the forest floor in a tangled heap.

I held onto her tightly as we fell, shielding her with my own body as the boar thundered past, its hot breath washing over us in a gust of fury. For a heartbeat, the world held its breath, the only sound the pounding of our hearts in unison.

Then, its massive form collided with a towering tree, sending a tremor through the forest floor. The impact reverberated through the air, causing the branches above to sway and creak in protest.

The creature seemed disoriented, its snarls replaced by confused grunts as it staggered backward, shaking its massive head to clear the haze of the collision. Elena and I watched in awe as the boar regained its footing, its dark eyes blazing with fury as it glared back at us.

It regained its composure, but I could see that the blow had taken its toll. The boar's movements were sluggish, its steps uncertain as it turned and lumbered away into the depths of the forest, disappearing into the shadows with a final grunt of frustration.

As the sounds of the creature's retreat faded into the distance, I let out a breath I hadn't realized I'd been holding, the tension draining from my muscles with each passing second. Beside me, Elena let out a shaky exhale, her fingers digging into my arm as she clung to me for support.

Relief washed over me in a wave, mingling with the lingering adrenaline that still pulsed through my veins.

As the rush of adrenaline faded, a bitter taste lingered in my mouth, replaced by the slow burn of anger. My muscles tensed, coiled like a spring ready to snap, as I replayed the scene in the forest over and over again in my mind.

The relief that initially washed over me evaporated, replaced by a seething fury that threatened to consume me whole. The image of Elena, vulnerable and defenseless, surrounded by the menacing presence of the boar, fueled the flames of my rage, igniting a primal instinct to protect and defend at all costs.

I couldn't shake the feeling of helplessness, the fear that gripped me in its icy embrace, as I realized just how close Elena came to danger.

The adrenaline that once masked my emotions served only to amplify them, the surge of energy coursing through my veins like a raging river. Every fiber of my being screamed with the need to lash out, to release the pent-up frustration that threatened to consume me from within.

With clenched fists and gritted teeth, I fought to keep my emotions in check, to channel the seething anger that simmered beneath the surface into something constructive. But it was like trying to contain a wildfire with nothing but bare hands, the flames licking hungrily at the edges, threatening to engulf me in their fury.

"Thank you," she whispered, sounding out of breath as she cradled her hurt leg.

Seeing her hurt and sounding so helpless was enough for me to blow everything out of proportion.

"What the hell were you thinking coming out all alone?" My voice was rising, but I didn't care. "You could have been killed!"

She looked down and remained silent. "Do you have enough sense to run when you see danger? Why did you stand there like a fool, waiting to be ripped apart?"

She looked up then, her fear replaced by anger. "Do you think I asked to be attacked by a boar? I'm not going to stand by and let you treat me like some helpless child. I can take care of myself, Logan. I don't need you acting like a hero."

"Oh really? That's how you see it? You don't know how foolish you were, standing around when you should have run." I couldn't bear to think of how right I was that I was a curse and having her around me wouldn't do her any good.

She struggled to her feet, anger clouding her face. "You know, if you were scared and afraid that I could have died, just say that. You don't need to hide your emotions with harsh words. You can just admit that I've come to mean something to you."

I scoffed and said words that I didn't intend. "Mean something to me? Maybe we are overplaying our parts here. I'm overplaying my part by saving you, and you're overplaying your part by assuming you know me and what I want."

Her words ignited a spark of anger within me, but it was fueled more by fear than anything else.

"What?"

"You heard me, Elena. You think you know me because we've had sex a few times; but you don't, and you're overplaying your part because of that."

The hurt expression that crossed Elena's face pierced through me like a knife, her pain cutting deeper than I could have anticipated.

Then she turned away silently, her shoulders slumped as she hobbled toward the cabin. As I watched her retreat, a part of me longed to reach out, to pull her back into my arms and never let her go.

But the fear that gripped me like a vice kept me rooted to the spot, unable to move, unable to bridge the ever-widening chasm between us. After a while, I turned around and went in the opposite direction, not ready to head back yet.

It was for the best.

8

Elena

"I'm overplaying my part?" I scoffed to myself for the umpteenth time as I stalked away from him. I was left to wonder if it was the same man who reassured me and planned a romantic dinner for me that I'd just left behind. The same one who was now saying something totally opposite.

I paused long enough to glance back at him to check if he was following, but he wasn't. He was walking in the opposite direction. Since he was obviously expecting me to go back to the cabin, in a moment of pure defiance, I turned away from the cabin and went into the forest instead.

The dense forest loomed around me, a tangle of ancient trees and shadowed paths that stretched endlessly into the distance. With each pain-filled step, my anger boiled inside me, a seething cauldron of frustration and resentment. Logan's arrogance was mind-blowing, almost like a discordant symphony.

The forest floor crunched beneath my heavy footsteps and makeshift walking stick, the rustle of leaves and snap of twigs a cacophony of sound that mirrored the tumultuous storm raging within me.

Memories of our argument replayed in my mind; how hard was it for him to admit that he was scared out of his wits? Why did he choose words that pierced my heart like daggers with their sharpness? His hard-headedness, his refusal to see beyond his own perspective—it was infuriating.

It wasn't like I wanted to be attacked by a boar. If anything, he was to be blamed; if he had allowed me to follow him, I would have been safe. Besides, he saved me and I was unscathed, even if the thought of the boar tearing me into shreds made me shiver.

What was more unbelievable was his assumption that I wanted something from him, that I expected anything because we'd slept with each other. Granted, I often give in to the fantasy of what might be, but I was no kid, and I knew how things worked. I hadn't allowed myself to imagine the extent of spending my life with him.

If anything, I wasn't certain if he would be leaving the forest; he had found his home and made every effort to make things comfortable for himself. He didn't appear to have any plan to move, so why would I plan out my future in the wilderness? How could he assume that I already was?

Maybe it was time to leave and give him the space he needed. I had my camera with me, and that was all that mattered. As I continued to navigate the winding trails, the natural beauty of the forest felt juxtaposed with my inner, tumultuous thoughts.

My anger became a driving storm, propelling me forward like a force of nature. I didn't stop to think about what would happen or what I would do if I ran into another boar. The thought was enough to deter me, but the need to prove a point urged me on.

The dense foliage enveloped me, its verdant embrace both comforting and stifling. Every breath was filled with the earthy scent of moss and decaying leaves, mingled with the crisp aroma of pine. I pushed through, branches scratching at my skin like desperate fingers, as if trying to hold me back.

I wasn't sure how long I'd been hobbling around, but every part of the forest was beginning to look the same. It stretched out before me like an endless labyrinth, each twist and turn a new challenge to overcome. But I didn't stop; my resolve only grew stronger, fueled by the fire of my anger.

I refused to think, maybe because I could feel the profound sadness beneath the anger—it came with the realization that what we had shared, however fleeting and exciting, was now slipping through my fingers like grains of sand. I couldn't believe that it had come to this, that our connection had been reduced to bitter words and hurtful accusations.

When I burst into a sudden clearing, I stilled as I tried to take in where I was. My eyes widened in shock at the scene before me. The once dense wilderness was marred by the presence of the men standing in front of me, four in number; their hands were busy callously destroying the forest.

Two of them were wielding axes, hacking away at the trees with reckless abandon, while the other two were setting snares and traps, probably to ensnare unsuspecting wildlife. The air was thick with the acrid scent of freshly cut wood and the metallic tang of blood, a stark contrast to the crisp, clean scent of pine needles I'd been inhaling throughout my walk.

Confusion clouded my mind as I tried to make sense of what I was seeing; as far as I knew, Logan had mentioned he was the only human living in these woods. These men were clearly up to no good, but it wasn't immediately apparent to me who they were or what they were doing.

The only group of people who would wreak havoc in a forest like this had to be poachers. My brain froze, and my eyes widened. I had heard stories of poachers and their illegal activities, but I had never come face to face with any before.

The reasonable thing to do would have been to turn around and run, or maybe hobble. I turned, and the makeshift walking stick clattered to the forest floor; it didn't make much noise since everywhere was carpeted with leaves, but it was enough to draw their attention.

As they noticed me, their faces twisted into sneers of contempt, and a chill ran down my spine. It was then that I realized the truth; they were indeed poachers, ruthless hunters who would stop at nothing to line their pockets with the spoils of their illegal trade.

Fear gripped my heart at the prospect of the danger I was in, but I knew I couldn't let them see my fear. With a deep breath, I forced myself to stand tall, my hands clenched into fists at my sides. I may have been alone and outnumbered, but I refused to let them intimidate me.

They stopped working and began to walk toward me. With each step they took closer, the tension in the air thickened, suffocating me with its palpable weight. I could feel their eyes boring into me, sizing me up like prey in a hunter's crosshairs. But I refused to back down, my jaw set in a defiant line as I met their gazes head-on.

I could feel their eyes stripping me bare, sizing me up like a piece of meat in a butcher's shop, and a knot of fear tightened in my chest as they began to close in on me. Their footsteps echoed through the stillness of the forest like an ominous drumbeat.

I knew I should run and escape while I still had the chance, but my legs refused to obey, rooted to the spot by a mixture of terror and defiance. I felt a surge of panic rise within me, threatening to overwhelm my senses. I could hear the pounding of my heart and my ragged breaths in my ears.

At the last moment, my body finally responded to my plea, and I turned around to hobble away as fast as I could. I had no sooner taken a few steps than someone's hands closed around my wrists with a vice-like grip. I struggled against their hold, but it was futile as their strength overpowered mine with ease.

Panic surged through me, and I struggled against their grasp. "Let me go!" I cried, my voice trembling. I was truly alone.

One of the poachers chuckled darkly, his eyes gleaming with malice. "Looks like we've stumbled upon a little spy," he sneered, tightening his grip on my wrists.

I recoiled at his words, my heart pounding in my chest. "I-I'm not a spy," I stammered, trying to keep my voice steady. "I was just hiking and... and I saw what you were doing."

The poacher's laugh was mocking, sending shivers down my spine. "Sure, you were," he said, his voice dripping with sarcasm. "And I suppose you weren't planning on reporting us to the authorities, were you? There's no better explanation as to why you're here alone so deep in the woods."

I swallowed hard, my mouth suddenly dry; I couldn't possibly tell them about Logan and put him in danger. "N-no," I whispered, "I just... I just wanted to get away."

The poachers exchanged knowing glances, and a cold knot formed in the pit of my stomach. They weren't listening, and they weren't about to let me go without a fight.

"Well, it's too late for that now," the poacher said, a cruel smile twisting his lips. "You've seen too much, sweetheart. Looks like you'll be coming with us."

Terror flooded through me as I realized the gravity of my situation. Trapped in the clutches of these ruthless men, I had no choice but to go along with them as they grabbed me. I prayed for a chance to escape before it was too late.

"Not so fast. We have to check out what we're going to be selling." One of the poachers stopped the other two who were dragging me. "You have to admit that we haven't seen one that would fetch such a good price before."

As he spoke, his hands came down to cup my breasts, squeezing them roughly as he thumbed my nipples. "Oh, fuck. I might have to sample her first."

He rough-handled me without mercy before leaning to sniff my neck. When his hands came down to rub against my pussy, my screams tore through the serene stillness of the forest, the primal, instinctual cry of fear and anguish.

The scream erupted from deep within me, a guttural sound that shattered the tranquility of the woods and echoed off the trees around me. It was followed by another, louder and more frantic, as panic surged through my veins like wildfire, fueling my fight for survival.

As I screamed, the poachers leered and jeered louder at me, and it only fueled my terror. Their mocking taunts twisted the knife of fear deeper into my heart. Their voices blended with the cacophony of the forest, creating a symphony of terror that surrounded me on all sides.

With each successive scream, my voice grew hoarse and ragged, the sound tearing through the air like a wounded animal's. Each cry carried with it a plea for salvation, a desperate call for someone, anyone, to come to my rescue. He continued to grope at me, heedless of my cries.

My pleas fell on deaf ears, drowned out by the raucous laughter of the poachers as they closed in on me with malicious intent. Their faces twisted into grotesque masks of amusement, their eyes gleaming with sadistic pleasure as they reveled in my fear.

"Look at her, boys, ain't she a feisty one?" one of them jeered, his voice dripping with malice as he reached out to grab me. "I reckon she'll fetch a pretty penny down at the market."

His words sent a chill down my spine, my heart pounding in my chest as I struggled against their relentless hold. But it was no use; they were too strong. Their grips were unyielding as they dragged me along like a helpless puppet on a string.

The forest seemed to close in around me, the trees looming ominously overhead as if bearing witness to my plight. With each step, I struggled not to succumb to the panic that threatened to suffocate me.

When I heard running feet thundering closer to where I was with the poachers, I thought it was my imagination playing tricks on me; surely, no one was close enough to rescue me.

Until I heard him say, "Let her go!" His voice rang out with an authority that brooked no argument, booming through the forest with a force that made the hardened poachers startle to a stop.

I managed to turn around and catch sight of him, large and imposing, as he stalked in our direction. My heart soared as he drew nearer, his rugged features set in a determined scowl that sent shivers down my spine.

I couldn't help but marvel at how effortlessly he moved, his powerful strides covering the ground with an ease that made my earlier frantic running seem clumsy and awkward in comparison.

Everything seemed to freeze as the poachers hesitated, uncertainty flickering in their eyes. But Logan didn't give them a chance to reconsider; his gaze locked on mine with a fierce intensity that made my heart race even faster.

"Did you not hear me? Get your dirty hands off her!" His eyes blazed with righteous fury, a tempest brewing behind their steely gaze as he bore down on the poachers with the force of a hurricane.

"Who the fuck are you?" The man who had been groping me stepped forward, trying to hide the shakiness in his voice. "Does the little slut have a man? You still have a chance to leave if you want to stay alive."

"Alright, I guess words don't work with you. Have it your way." His silhouette cut a striking figure against the backdrop of the forest, his form outlined by the dappled sunlight filtering through the canopy above.

And then, like a bolt from the blue, Logan burst into action, racing toward the men with a scowl. Caught off guard by his sudden rush, the poachers faltered and scrambled to face him.

Their bravado crumbled like sandcastles in the tide as they scrambled to release me from their grasp, their faces contorted in fear, probably at the thought of what may happen to them.

With a primal roar that echoed through the forest, Logan hurled himself toward them, his movements fluid and precise like a seasoned warrior facing his foes. His fists moved with blinding speed as they connected with the poachers, each blow landing with a satisfying crunch.

The poachers staggered backward; their faces twisted in a mixture of shock and disbelief. I stood transfixed, my heart pounding in my chest as I watched him fight four men bravely without faltering. He moved with a grace that belied his size and strength. His every movement was a symphony of precision and power.

He easily held his ground against them, with speed and agility, as he deftly dodged their attacks and launched devastating counterstrikes. Everything sped up and seemed to happen in a blur.

One moment, the men were charging at him, and in the next, Logan delivered final, decisive blows that sent the poachers sprawling to the forest floor in defeat. With an animalistic roar, he remained crouched, waiting for any of them to get up, his chest heaving with exertion as he surveyed them.

"Never come here again," he said through clenched teeth when it became obvious that they wouldn't be getting up again.

With a swift motion, he closed the gap between us, his strong arms wrapping around me protectively as he pulled me close. I felt safe and secure in his embrace, my fear and uncertainty melting away in the warmth of his presence. I didn't struggle when he scooped me up and began to walk toward the cabin.

As he walked, I remembered how the men touched me and I couldn't help but feel a wave of disgust wash over me. Their touch felt invasive, like insects crawling beneath my skin, leaving a trail of revulsion in their wake. Every graze of their fingers left a lingering feeling of contamination, as if their mere presence had tainted me in some irreparable way.

I clenched my teeth, fighting back the bile rising in my throat at the memory of the way their lecherous gazes bore into me, stripping away any semblance of dignity or autonomy.

My skin crawled with an overwhelming sense of repulsion, and I longed to scrub away the filth that lingered on my body.

"Are you okay?" Logan asked when I tensed up in his arms. "Did they hurt you?"

"They touched me," I managed to say, burying my face into his chest. "I need you, Logan." I needed him to burn away the memory from my brain.

He hesitated when he understood the meaning of my words. "I don't think..." he began; he was obviously going to turn me down.

I stopped him by pressing my lips against his, glad that he was warm, moist, and accepting. I kissed Logan passionately as if I hadn't kissed him in over a decade. I ran my hands up and down his rippling back. The touch of his skin beneath my hands drove me wild, like a drug that infused me with pure lust.

I looked up at him, needing him to understand the depth of my wish and desire.

"Please," I begged as he moved me in his arms to secure a better hold.

"Do you really want me to?" Logan asked and held me tighter as if to convince me otherwise.

"Yes, please."

"Let's get inside then."

There was no need for foreplay or romance; I wanted him deep inside me to feel every inch of him and convince myself that it had all been a terrible nightmare. He seemed to understand perfectly; he placed me on the bed so I was lying face down.

I wasn't wet, but I was ready for him. We were both fully clad when he thrust inside me with one swift movement; I didn't expect to feel pleasure. My eyes rolled back, and I dropped my head down at the brutality of the force that seized my body, both painful and blissful.

I didn't feel like I was being taken advantage of as he drove in and out of me with reckless abandon. Deep down, I craved the kind of animalistic pleasure Logan was giving me.

There was no need to think about what would be, no worry about our previous argument, and no need to think about his hurtful words. I decided that I just needed to be fucked out of my mind. No relationship. No warm-and-fuzzies. No expectations. No commitment. Just raw, carnal, intense sex.

Logan's hands pressed me into the bed as he continued to fuck me roughly. His touch against my skin filled me with a sort of electric euphoria that seemed to shoot sinuously to my throbbing pussy.

My heart pounded in my heaving chest. I felt energized. I felt safer than ever before. My pussy burned with lust, wetness dripped from my core, and I wanted more.

Logan was a relentless lover when he wanted to be. He was fast, then slow, cold, then passionate, and I felt a deep hunger from him. It was as if he hadn't had a woman in years and couldn't help but unleash all he had on me.

My body was more than eager to be the victim of his painful pleasure. I lifted myself up so my ass was in the air, and I was on my knees, meeting his thrust as he continued to pump in and out with supernatural power.

Just when I thought my pussy couldn't handle any more drilling, I heard Logan start to groan. His guttural groan sent shivers up my spine and made my pussy clench around his pumping dick as I milked him for all he had.

His finishing thrusts were harder than the rest; each hard thrust nearly knocked the wind out of me and forced me forward, back on my chest, eating the sheets. His body went completely tight, and he cried out in passion.

When it was over, I collapsed onto the bed fully, tears streaming from my eyes as sleep finally came. Blissful and sweet.

9

LOGAN

I'd never been the type to dally or waste time on what could be, but I couldn't help wondering what would have happened if I hadn't decided to follow Elena at the last minute or how things would have spiraled out of control if I hadn't gotten there in time to rescue her from those men.

The soft glow of the setting sun cast a gold sheen across the cabin, bathing everything in a gentle, bright light. I stood at the edge of the bed, watching Elena sleep peacefully, her chest rising and falling in a steady rhythm. I felt a bit sad that I'd handled her roughly, even if she didn't seem to mind.

She looked so serene, so vulnerable in the quiet of the evening, so different from the pure horror I saw on her face when those men mishandled her, and I couldn't help but feel a surge of protectiveness wash over me.

I gazed down at her, and memories of the events that had led me here flooded my mind, each one more vivid than the last. I remembered the panic that had gripped me when I realized she hadn't returned to the cabin, the frantic search through the forest as I called out her name relentlessly.

When I heard her scream, it felt like déjà vu; it was the second time I had heard it in a day, yet this scream sounded different. There was a tinge of desperation and absolute panic that sent a shiver down my spine.

I could feel the adrenaline coursing through my veins as I ran through the trees, the branches scraping against my skin as I pushed myself to go faster, to find her before it was too late.

Every step was a battle against time, against the fear that I would be too late to save her. I could hear the pounding of my own heart in my ears, the rhythm matching the frantic pace of my footsteps as I raced through the forest, searching for any sign of her presence.

And then, just when I feared I would never find her, I saw her struggling against the vile men, her leg bleeding as they dragged her along with them. Relief flooded through me like a tidal wave, washing away the fear and uncertainty that had plagued me since the moment she disappeared, but it only lasted for a moment.

Anger clouded every other emotion when I saw the greed and lust in the eyes of those men. I refused to think about what they would have done to her if I hadn't arrived on time. Everything else passed in a blur and by the time it was all over, only the ache in my muscles, the slight cuts, and the men trembling on the floor, reassured me that it had happened.

The moment I reached out to her, my fingers brushed against her skin as I pulled her into my arms, holding her close to reassure myself that she was real and that she was safe. It was one of the most clarifying moments in my life. I knew how close I had come to losing her, the same way I'd lost everything else that mattered to me.

But as I looked down at her, peaceful, and unharmed, I knew that I would do it all again in a heartbeat. Because, in the end, keeping her safe was all that mattered, even if it meant facing my own demons in the process.

Is that really all that matters? the sneaky and snarky voice at the back of my head asked. *How long do you think you can keep her safe before she ends up like your mother, father, dead girlfriend, and the people you served with?*

I shook my head, trying to shut the voice up, but it was too late. I was already back to the day when my father died.

I remembered the hushed stillness of the hospital room, how I sat, watchful, by my father's bedside, and how his once-strong hand now felt feeble in my grasp. The warmth that used to radiate from his touch waned like the dying embers of a once-roaring fire.

It was a surreal moment, watching him slip away before my eyes, his breaths growing shallower with each passing second. I felt powerless, like a lone ship tossed in a stormy sea, unable to steer a course or find refuge from the relentless waves of sorrow crashing over me.

Part of me was relieved that his suffering would soon come to an end, but another part was consumed by guilt and regret. Why wasn't I there when he needed me most? Why did I leave him alone, even for just a moment?

I was haunted by the knowledge that I hadn't been there for him, that I'd missed his final words because I chose to go home for a change of clothes and shower.

I held his hand and I couldn't help but wonder if he felt abandoned, if he resented me for not being by his side in his final conscious moments. The thought gnawed at me, filling me with a profound sense of loss and longing. I wished I could turn back time and rewrite the script of our final chapter together, but I knew that was impossible.

I grappled with my emotions, wrestling with conflicting feelings of sorrow, guilt, and resentment. It was a tangled web of feelings, impossible to unravel as I sat by his side, silently mourning the impending loss of my father and grappling with the uncertain future that lay ahead.

The moment when he finally lost the battle against cancer was surreal, and I can still remember everything in detail. The waning warmth slowly faded, replaced by an icy chill that seeped into my bones, mirroring the cold emptiness that settled in the depths of my soul.

I remembered watching helplessly as his breaths grew shallower, each one a painful reminder of the life slipping away. How tears streamed down my cheeks unchecked, falling on his cold body. I couldn't forget whispering a tearful farewell and telling him I didn't resent him for leaving me behind in a world suddenly devoid of light and warmth.

The months after his death passed in a haze. I went through the motions of sleeping, waking, eating, and managing the business, but I wasn't truly living. At least, until I met Willow.

Willow had a bubbly energy and infectious warmth that drew me to her like a moth; our love was at first sight and mutual. I immediately asked her to be my girlfriend, and she agreed to be after we went on ten dates, and if she still loved me.

Those were the most colorful and happiest moments of my life. I opened up to her and believed I could finally have a chance at happiness. Little did I know I would lose her on the night of our tenth date, right after she told me she would marry me if I bought her a ring and was still in love with her.

I wished I hadn't been so over the moon with happiness. I immediately told her to wait while I ran to the nearest jewelry store. I wanted everything to be perfect for her; maybe if I hadn't called her excitedly on my way back while flashing the ring, she might still be alive.

One moment, she was waving back at me with all smiles; the next, she was hit by an oncoming truck, and her wave stilled. I rushed forward, in the haunting stillness of the night. I held her close, her fragile form cradled against my chest.

Her fading warmth was a bittersweet reminder of the life slipping away beneath my trembling hands, the same way my father had passed. The pavement beneath us felt cold and unforgiving, a cruel contrast to the remaining warmth of her presence that I desperately clung to.

Time seemed to slow to a crawl, each passing moment stretching into eternity as I watched helplessly. My heart ached with pain so raw it felt like it might tear me apart. The world around us was hushed; the only sound was the distant echo of sirens piercing the silence like a mournful lament.

With shaking hands, I traced the lines of her face, memorizing every curve and contour as if trying to etch her image into my mind forever. Her once vibrant eyes, now clouded with pain and fear, met mine with a silent plea that cut me to the core, begging for comfort that I was powerless to provide.

As her breaths grew shallow and labored, I leaned in close, pressing my lips against her forehead in a tender kiss. My voice was a broken whisper of love and desperation as I pleaded with her to hold on, to fight against the darkness threatening to consume her.

I could feel her slipping away with each passing moment, with each faltering breath she took, tearing me apart with a pain I could not bear. I yelled for the ambulance and for help. But they never arrived on time.

Willow's last words were, "I love you." Then she took her last breath.

In the agonizing silence that followed, I held her tighter, clinging to her with all the strength I had left, unwilling to let her go even as I felt her slipping away from me. As her eyelids fluttered closed for the final time, I whispered a tearful farewell, my voice choked with grief and despair as I watched her slip away into the darkness, leaving me alone in a world suddenly devoid of light and hope once again.

The thought of her death pushed me into depression, and I tried many times to take my own life, but I always failed. It was what pushed me to enroll in military service and sign up to be at the front line; I was seducing death, telling him to take me to those I'd lost.

Months later, death truly answered my calls. However, he didn't come for me; he came for everyone else in my unit. I could still feel the heat of the blast, the deafening roar that had torn through the air like thunder, leaving chaos and destruction in its wake.

The acrid stench of smoke and burning debris filled my nostrils, choking me with its bitter taste. I could hear the screams of the wounded and the frantic shouts of my fellow soldiers as they searched for survivors amidst the carnage.

I can remember trying to clear my head and helping them when another bomb went off. It set my ears ringing with echoes of the explosion, and I succumbed to claws of unconsciousness.

By the time I came to, I was buried under a pile of rubble; I can almost taste the metallic tang of blood on my tongue even now and feel the searing heat of the harsh sun beating down on my skin. Everywhere was eerily silent.

I remembered clawing my way out, and the first thing I saw was my fallen comrades, their expressions frozen in death as if accusing me of survival while they had perished. I couldn't remember how long I was trapped there without food or water.

I was told after I was found that they'd been searching for survivors for an entire week, and I was the only one remaining.

"Logan?" Elena's voice and soft touch jolted me back; I was so shocked that I almost bolted away. "Are you okay?"

I rubbed my face, trying to rein in my thoughts. "Yes, I'm fine." I sounded brusque and uncaring, but I didn't want to worry about that at the moment.

"You must be so angry; I'm sorry I made you worry by going off on my own. I won't do that again." I stared down at her, willing myself to feel something. Maybe anger or resentment, but there was nothing.

Only indifference and a blank mind.

"I'm not angry," I finally said. "But I think it would be better if you leave as soon as your leg heals; it will be better if neither of us gets too attached." That was the only way she could remain safe.

I pretended not to notice the oppressive silence that suddenly filled the room. I avoided looking at Elena, unable to bear the weight of her gaze as she watched me with those troubled eyes of hers.

"I need a break," I said, finally, and stepped out of the cabin, hoping she would have enough sense to stay in and not go looking for trouble.

I walked with purpose, my footsteps echoing in the silence of the forest as I made my way deeper into the woods. I told myself that it was for the best, that pushing Elena away was the only way to protect her from the cold hands of death that were already struggling to get to her.

By the time I realized how far I'd walked, I was already at the spot where I had confronted the poachers earlier, and to my satisfaction, they were gone. The only thing that hinted at their presence was the hacked trees and blood from killed animals.

As I continued to survey the area, my gaze fell upon something lying half-buried in the undergrowth. Curiosity piqued, I moved closer and reached down to retrieve it, my fingers closing around the familiar shape of Elena's camera.

A wave of emotion washed over me as I held the camera in my hands, memories of Elena flooding my mind. Out of curiosity, I turned on the camera to check the photos she had taken; I was struck by the beauty and skill captured in each image.

The forest came alive before my eyes through the lens; I could easily see her talent and passion for photography, even as an amateur. From the play of light and shadow to the intricate details of the natural world, her photos were a window into a world I had never fully appreciated until now.

As I continued to scroll through the images, I couldn't help but tear up; they were the most beautiful things I'd ever seen. They were so untouched by the ugliness of the world.

Hold on, why was I crying?

10

ELENA

It would have been better if he'd been mad at me; something about the way he calmly said, 'I'm not angry. But I think it would be better if you leave as soon as your leg heals; it will be better if neither of us gets too attached,' scared the heck out of me.

It almost felt like he was too drained and tired and didn't even have the energy to get mad at me. It was as if I wouldn't understand what he meant, no matter how much he explained, and maybe he was right. I'd been trying to think about everything that had happened, but I still didn't get why he treated me so coldly.

The cabin was cloaked in a hushed stillness as I sat alone; the only sound was the soft crackle of the dying embers in the fireplace. The warmth of the fire did little to chase away the chill that settled over me, a reminder of the icy silence that had descended between Logan and me before he left.

As I gazed into the flickering flames, my thoughts drifted back to our earlier confrontation, the sharp sting of his coldness still fresh in my mind. Part of me wished he had lashed out in anger; his fiery temper would have been a welcome contrast to the frosty distance he had chosen instead.

I couldn't shake the feeling of regret that gnawed at my insides, a heavy weight that hung over me like a dark cloud. In truth, I had acted impulsively, driven by wounded pride and hurt feelings, and now I found myself grappling with the consequences of my actions.

Left alone with my thoughts, a new perspective began to take shape—the encounter with the poachers and the danger I had faced was enough to make anyone run mad, and it was what probably forced me to confront the truth about Logan.

Despite our differences, despite the walls he had erected around himself, he had risked everything to protect me, a stranger he barely knew. Having sex didn't warrant him risking his life for me twice, which could only mean one thing. He was a kind man through and through.

The realization washed over me like a wave, filling me with a newfound sense of awe and appreciation for the man who had come to my rescue. I understood just how amazing Logan truly was, his selflessness and bravery shining through every time I was in danger.

I needed to find a way to make things right with Logan, to bridge the gap that had grown between us. Because in the end,

I knew that we were stronger together than we ever could be apart.

The walls I had erected around my heart began to crumble; the barriers of pride and hurt melted away in the warmth of newfound understanding. I realized then that Logan's silence was probably not a sign of indifference but rather a reflection of his own inner turmoil.

But I also knew that it didn't matter how much I wanted to make things right; I couldn't push him, at least not until he was ready. If I pushed against him too much, he would probably bolt.

It hurt to be held at arms-length by him. It annoyed me to wait uselessly when we could be discussing what was wrong, and it was difficult to hold my impatience at bay. Still, I had to give him the space he required to calm himself and his emotions before approaching.

I looked outside. The sun already set and it would soon be nightfall, but he wasn't back. I hoped he would be back before I fell asleep again. I glanced around, wondering what I could do to keep myself busy.

I wished I could cook and give him a break from cooking for both of us, but I didn't want to burn the cabin down. I hobbled around, remaking the bed and clearing away the trash. By the time I was done, I still felt restless; that was when I remembered my camera.

We didn't stop to take it back with us, and I wondered if the poachers had grabbed it. I got to my feet; I needed to check. The camera was too important.

I hesitated at the last moment, remembering that Logan was yet to be back. He might worry if he returned and found me gone, and I wondered if I wouldn't be getting myself into trouble going all alone into the woods again.

I shook my head. I would have to be careful this time and leave a note so he wouldn't worry. Fingers trembling slightly, I reached for a piece of paper, the rough texture scraping against my skin as I hastily retrieved it from the cluttered table.

With a pen gripped tightly in my hand, I began to scrawl out a note. "I went to look for my camera," I wrote. "Don't worry, I'll be back soon; I know exactly where it is."

As I read over the note, a wave of uncertainty washed over me. Would Logan understand my need to look for the camera, or would he see it as being senseless of me after almost getting kidnapped? The thought lingered in the back of my mind as I folded the note and left it on the table for him to find.

I stepped outside into the cool evening air. Darkness was slowly enveloping the forest like a cloak, and I knew I had to make haste—the memory of danger was still fresh in my mind. The forest, which I once regarded as a place of solace and beauty, now seemed ominous and foreboding, each shadow and rustle a potential threat lurking in the darkness.

Despite the sense of unease, I pressed on, my footsteps echoing softly on the forest floor as I hobbled and limped around in search of my lost camera. The twilight offered some guidance as I navigated through the woods, my senses on high alert for any sign of danger.

I couldn't shake the feeling of vulnerability that lingered in the air as I moved deeper into the woods, a constant reminder of the danger I had narrowly escaped. What if I came across something else that was worse than a boar or a group of poachers? What would I do?

The sense of unease strengthened as I made my way along the path; the memory of their hands all over my body almost made me puke. Each step felt heavier than the last, weighed down by my conflicting emotions and the uncertainty of what lay ahead.

But just as I rounded a bend in the trail and came out of the familiar clearing, my heart leaped into my throat as I caught sight of Logan ahead. He was crouched over on his knees; his shoulders were shaking, and he appeared to be holding something. It took me a while to realize that he was crying.

My heart slowed to a stop. Logan? Crying? Why? Since when? How could I help? Should I leave? Would he want to be comforted? Would he prefer to be left alone? The questions almost made me turn around and hide or go back to the cabin. But I couldn't; I was rooted in that spot.

Logan was usually so strong, manly, and composed, so the sight of him falling apart uncontrollably brought tears to my own eyes. His whole frame seemed to tremble with the force of his crying, each sob wracking his body as if he were being torn apart from within.

It was a raw and vulnerable display, one that spoke volumes of the pain he was harboring deep within his soul. As I drew closer, I could hear the ragged hitch in his breath, the gut-wrenching sound of his anguish echoing through the stillness of the forest.

His cries were a symphony of heartbreak, each note piercing through the darkness and reverberating in the depths of my own being. I reached out tentatively, my fingers brushing against his trembling form as if to offer some small measure of solace.

But he seemed oblivious to my touch, lost in the depths of his despair as tears streamed unchecked down his cheeks. I longed to comfort him, to take away the pain that was making him suffer.

When I could no longer watch, I knelt beside him and hugged him tightly from the back; my eyes fell on the object cradled in his hands. It took a moment for my mind to register what I was seeing, but when recognition finally dawned, my breath caught in my throat.

There, in his grasp, was my camera. I couldn't believe I had forgotten all about it when I saw him. I wondered if he came down intentionally to retrieve the camera for me and if the reason he was crying was because he remembered the danger I was in.

It was all an assumption; I would only know why he was crying when he told me. For what felt like an eternity, we remained locked in that silent embrace; the only sound was the haunting echo of Logan's grief ringing through the trees.

I continued to hold him close; it was the least I could do since he had done so much for me. It was a side of him I had never seen before, and the sight of his pain tore at my heartstrings in a way I couldn't ignore.

"What's wrong?" I whispered softly when his tears slowed, my voice barely above a hush as I pressed closer to him. My injured leg was screaming for relief, but I ignored it. "You can tell me whatever is wrong; I'm sorry if it's because I made you risk your life."

For a long moment, he didn't respond, his tears continuing to fall unchecked as he clung to me like a lifeline. But eventually, he pulled away slightly, his gaze meeting mine with a mixture of vulnerability and pain.

"It's... it's nothing," he murmured, his voice choked with emotion. But even as he spoke the words, I could see the truth written plainly in his eyes—there was something, and he felt reluctant to say it.

I shook my head gently. "No, it's not nothing," I insisted, my tone firm but gentle. "You don't have to carry this burden alone, Logan. Please tell me."

He looked up at me, his eyes red and swollen from crying, and held out the camera, showing me the photos I had taken.

"It's these pictures," he said, his voice trembling with emotion. "They're the most beautiful things I've ever seen."

"What?" Out of everything I was expecting him to say, that wasn't it.

I couldn't help but be taken aback by his words. After everything he had been through, I hadn't expected him to be moved by something as simple as photographs of nature.

"I'm glad you like them." I finally said.

But Logan shook his head, a sad smile playing at the corners of his lips. "You don't understand. It's not just about liking them," he said, his voice barely above a whisper.

"It's... it's everything. After all the horrors I've seen, these images remind me that there's still beauty in the world. That there's still something worth fighting for."

"What?" I was still confused and thrown.

"You probably don't understand, right? But the truth is, if you had seen what I have, you may have wanted to give up. But these pictures remind me that there's still something worth holding on to."

I gaped, unable to say a word, and continued hearing him talk.

"Those pictures represent hope, warmth, the simple joy of life, and that there are still second chances, at least to me."

"You could sense all of that from these?" I couldn't believe it; the pictures were still raw and unedited, yet he felt everything

I'd always wanted someone to experience when they looked at my work.

Tears welled up in my eyes as the weight of his words sank into my soul. His heartfelt observations washed over me like a gentle breeze; I felt a rush of emotions swirling within me, like leaves caught in a whirlwind.

I was floored by his words. It was as if he had reached into the depths of my soul and plucked out my deepest desires, laying them bare for the world to see. To hear him express such profound appreciation for my work was both surprising and humbling, and I struggled to find the right words to respond.

He wouldn't know how much his words meant to me and just how much I'd been hoping to hear someone say that. It was what I lived for, and it washed away the snide remarks from those women; maybe my journey into the woods wasn't a coincidence after all.

I realized just how much I wanted people to see the world through my lens – to find beauty and solace in the natural world, even amid darkness and despair.

Maybe meeting Logan was predestined; without a word, I wrapped my arms around him, pulling him close in an embrace. It was as if he had peeled back the layers of my carefully constructed facade, revealing the raw essence of who I truly was.

Someday in the future, I would probably have enough courage to open up to him and tell him what he gave me at that moment.

11

LOGAN

"Why are you crying, too?" I asked when I felt her tears seep in through my shirt.

As the intensity of the moment began to fade, I became acutely aware of the vulnerability I had just displayed. Embarrassment washed over me like a sudden downpour, leaving me feeling exposed and foolish in the wake of my emotional outburst.

I cursed myself inwardly for allowing my guard to slip, for revealing a side of myself that I had always worked so hard to conceal. It made me wonder if she was crying so I could feel better about crying.

"You wouldn't understand," she sniffled and continued holding me tightly.

My cheeks flushed with heat as I wiped away the lingering traces of tears; I couldn't help but feel a sense of shame wash over me. I chastised myself for allowing Elena to see me in such a raw and unguarded state, for exposing the cracks in the armor I had worn so proudly for so long.

"Is it because I asked you to leave as soon as your leg heals?" I asked again, wondering what I would say if her answer was yes.

But she shook her head. "It's not that, but my leg is killing me right now. I've been using it for support for so long."

A surge of concern shot through me like a bolt of lightning, overriding any other emotions that might have been brewing beneath the surface. I sprang into action, my instincts kicking into high gear as I focused all my attention on her leg.

A surge of anger simmered just below the surface, a flash of frustration at the thought of her pushing herself too hard, too soon. But I pushed it aside, knowing that now was not the time for recriminations, and yelling at her would probably lead to another argument.

Instead, I focused on what needed to be done, my movements swift and decisive as I bundled her gently and walked over to the nearest tree that had been hacked by the foolish men, settling her to sit on my lap.

As she settled against me and gave a sigh of relief, I couldn't help but feel a pang of guilt for not noticing her discomfort sooner. I glanced down and noticed her entire leg was swollen. I swore inwardly for allowing my own emotions to cloud my judgment, for failing to see past my own turmoil to recognize her needs.

I began to massage her legs, my fingers tracing the contours of her skin with a gentle yet purposeful touch; I couldn't help but be struck by the softness and femininity of her form. Each stroke sent a shiver of sensation racing through me, igniting a primal need that surged to life.

Her skin felt smooth beneath my fingertips, the warmth of her body seeping into my own with every caress. It was an intimate act, and it stirred something wild and untamed deep within me.

She gave a soft moan of approval as she sagged against me, and I immediately felt a growing tension building in the pit of my stomach, a hunger that demanded to be sated. It was a feeling unlike anything I had ever experienced before; after sleeping together numerous times, a moan from her shouldn't have affected me so much.

Desire coursed through my veins like wildfire, and I continued to force myself to focus on the task at hand, to push aside the maelstrom of emotions that was making me hard under her lap. I could only hope it didn't poke at her.

"So, you're a photographer?" I asked to take my attention away from the bolt of need.

"Hmm," she answered noncommittally, her eyes closed; she was clinging to my shoulders.

"Do you only deal with wildlife photography?" I asked again, wishing she would stop making the little sounds in her throat.

"Hmm, that feels amazing," she purred like a satisfied cat again. I pressed a little harder to bring back her focus. "Oh no, I only recently got into wildlife photography. I also do landscape, astrophotography, and portraits."

"Really?" I felt a surge of pride. "So you recently got into wildlife photography, and you're this good?" It made me wonder about the kind of life she'd led out of these woods and in her comfort zone.

I would have asked, but something held me back, maybe for fear that she would ask similar questions.

"So, you were into the military, too? When did you leave?" she asked casually, and I tensed before forcing myself to relax.

"I was discharged two years ago." Which reminded me that it had been over a year since I'd lived in the woods, and never looked back.

"Oh." She nodded, but I could feel her tensing up, and I wondered why.

The next question she asked gave me the answer.

"You mentioned the horrors you witnessed in the army. Do you mind sharing?"

I tensed again, but this time I couldn't bring myself to release the tension. Yes, I did mind, but she was looking at me so expectantly, and for the life of me, I couldn't deny her.

"When I joined the army, I volunteered to be on the front line." I held my breath, praying she wouldn't ask why, and thankfully, she didn't. "I witnessed a lot of my fellow soldiers being shot dead on the spot, and we would have to move on, leaving them behind, hoping they would retrieve the bodies on time so the wild animals wouldn't feed on them."

I drew in a deep breath, "Have you ever heard the last breath someone takes before they die? The horrendous scream of pain, the nauseating sight of blood flowing, the gory way the body twists when someone is blown to pieces."

It was her turn to gasp, but that wasn't even a quarter of the things I'd seen on the front line. "The sounds of guns firing close to your ears without protection, inhaling the smell of rotten flesh from wounded legs stuck into combat boots for weeks, rationing food so you don't starve, and the nightmares that follow. They are unspeakable."

"I think I like you better when you aren't scaring me," Elena said and buried her face into my neck. I knew she meant to be funny, but I wondered if she would go running for the hills if she found out the full story.

It was probably time to switch up the topic again; in truth, I'd opened up to her in ways I never thought possible. It was the most I'd ever spoken about my experiences in the military.

"Listen, Elena," I began, telling myself that since I already showed her a vulnerable part of myself, it wouldn't hurt to go a step further. "I know I said I wanted you to leave as soon as your leg heals; I hope you don't take it the wrong way."

"Logan..." she began, but I cut her off.

"Let me finish." She nodded. "The truth is, anything you see me do is for your own benefit, and I won't deny that I need solitude. But I've come to realize that I need you too; you've made things better with your presence, and I was lying when I said I wanted to see you leave."

I drew in another breath, "I want you more than I've wanted anything in the world, and I'm not so sure I would like for you to leave as soon as you can. I mean, I don't want others around, but I want you around. I don't...." I realized I was starting to ramble, trying to explain myself.

Elena raised a hand to my lips. "I understand what you mean, and it's fine if you don't have everything figured out just yet. You still have until my leg heals to make a decision; you don't have to rush things."

"Elena..." I said, my throat tightening with emotions.

"Shush, stop scaring me and kiss me." Her words were enough to make all the blood in my head flow into my dick. "Don't pretend you don't want this; I can feel you."

"If I kiss you, it won't stop at a kiss," I warned, wondering if she wasn't too sore for what I had in mind. After all, I had fucked her earlier, hard and fast.

"Who says I want it to stop at a kiss? A kiss can't handle what I can feel against my ass." I'd never heard her talk so bluntly before, and I started to believe I still had a long way to go before I knew the real Elena.

"Well, you will have to do this work this time." *You're such a sucker for her*, a voice taunted in my head, *one minute you want her gone, and the next, you want to get into her pants.*

Drawing in a long breath, I exhaled slowly, trying to steady my racing pulse.

"What do you want me to do?" Elena's question hung in the air, her eyes locked on mine with a mixture of anticipation and uncertainty.

"Seriously?" I couldn't help but ask, a hint of amusement tugging at the corners of my lips; this would be more enjoyable than I thought.

"I want to see you. All of you in this twilight," I said.

Pursing her lips, she got down from my lap and limped to stand in front of me. She was wearing one of my shirts, and it came down to the top of her knees; it was arousing to see her in my clothes.

She raised her arms over her chest and peeled off the shirt in one fluid motion with a mischievous glint in her eyes. My breath caught in my throat as her breasts came into view, barely contained by the lacy bra she wore, the same one she was wearing the day I found her.

I licked my lips in anticipation, imagining what lay beneath the frilly temptation. The flirty and sensual atmosphere was in contrast to the emotional and tense atmosphere of earlier, and I was learning that, with Elena, I had to take things in stride.

She kicked off her shoes and stood barefoot on the fallen leaves; I couldn't tear my gaze away, my eyes tracing the curves of her body as she wiggled out of her pants. Standing before me in nothing but a sweet little pair of panties that matched her bra, she made my blood run as hot as molten lava.

"Let me see your breasts," I asked, my voice husky with desire, unable to contain the longing in my tone. It was hard to believe I sounded like that.

"What if someone passes by?" she asked as she reached behind her to unhook her bra, her movements hesitant but determined.

"We are alone," I assured her.

Swallowing hard, I watched as her breasts fell free from the lacy cups, the thin satin straps slipping down her arms with a tantalizing slowness. I couldn't tear my gaze away, transfixed by the sight of her, my heart pounding in my chest. It felt like I hadn't seen her before.

She tucked her bottom lip between her teeth, a gesture that sent a jolt of desire straight to my core. In one swift movement, she slid her panties over her hips, down her legs, and stepped out of them, leaving her completely exposed before me.

My gaze lingered on the neatly trimmed patch of hair at the junction of her thighs, my mouth suddenly dry with anticipation. I licked my lips, remembering the taste of her on my tongue, the memory sending a surge of heat through me.

She limped forward and sank down to her knees beside me; my pulse quickened and my breath came in shallow gasps as she reached for the fly of my jeans. I looked up at her, unable to find my voice, as she flicked open the button and ran my zipper down.

"Your leg, isn't it hurting?" I managed to ask, but she shook her head.

When she reached inside my pants and pulled out my dick, I couldn't suppress the groan that escaped my lips. I almost thought she would take me in her mouth. But before I could fully comprehend what was happening, she stood and backed into me, placing her weight on her leg as she lifted her ass to straddle my hips. She lowered herself onto my dick and her warmth enveloped me in a sensation that was almost overwhelming.

My fear about her being sore disappeared; she was ready. More than ever.

"Gently," I managed to croak, my voice strained with desire and restraint. I was consumed by a mixture of arousal and concern, wanting nothing more than to lose myself in her but also desperate to ensure her comfort and pleasure.

I sucked in a ragged breath, my fingers tightening on her thighs as she enveloped me completely. The sensation was electrifying, sending waves of pleasure coursing through me as she began to move, her hips rotating in a slow, tantalizing rhythm.

"Oh fuck," I moaned, unable to contain the pleasure that washed over me with each movement of her body. I guided her movements with my hands, unable to resist the urge to lift her hips and thrust up to meet her.

I was consumed by a blissful haze of pleasure, my senses overwhelmed by the exquisite sensation of her body against mine. I was straining to hold back my release, wanting nothing more than to prolong the ecstasy of the moment for as long as possible.

She looked back at me, her tongue sweeping over her lips; I groaned in desperation, my control slipping with each passing second. I knew I couldn't hold on much longer; the overwhelming need to release was building to an unbearable intensity.

Sweat was beading my forehead, dripping down my sides as the intensity of our union threatened to overwhelm me. When she leaned against me so I could support her weight, her back rubbing against my chest, the added pressure on my dick was nearly my undoing.

But she reached the peak first. Her body stiffened, and her eyes widened as her pussy rippled on my aching dick. I watched as she let her head fall back, her nipples pointing to the sky, and she made the sweetest little squeaking sound deep in her throat as she reached the peak of her pleasure.

And came.

But she didn't stop moving.

Her body undulated against mine, her movements driving me to the brink of ecstasy. I put my hands on her hips, trying to still her, but the sensations coursing through me were too powerful to resist.

With a primal instinct and without warning, I pushed hard into her body as my dick leaped, and jets of release poured from me into her warm, slick pussy. Staring up at her, I saw her shudder, her eyes glazed with the intensity of our shared passion.

Her beautiful lips were parted, her breath coming in ragged gasps as she slowly lowered her hips for the last time, for the last spurt of cum leaving my body as my dick ceased to flex.

We lay there for the longest time, naked as the day we were born, trying to even out our breathing.

"That was perfect," I whispered and finally kissed her.

12

ELENA

"I can't believe I will have a creature so pretty and innocent in my stomach a few hours from now," I grumbled and looked at Logan accusingly.

"Oh, shush. You're only complaining because you are seeing them before they are cooked. Now, focus, unless you want us to go to bed without food."

I sighed and did as I was told; my stomach was already rumbling. So much for skipping breakfast because we had been too busy making the bed creak.

As we crouched behind a cluster of bushes, the anticipation hung heavy in the air, mingling with the earthy scent of the forest. Logan's hand signaled for me to stay still, his eyes scanning the clearing ahead with unwavering focus.

I nodded silently, my heart pounding in my chest as we waited for our prey to appear, trusting him to do his magic. The forest around us seems to hold its breath, every rustle and chirp amplified in the hushed atmosphere. I held my breath, too, my senses on high alert, as if willing the rabbit to reveal itself.

Minutes stretched into eternity, and I forced myself to remain still. When my stomach grumbled loudly and Logan's gaze flickered to mine, a ghost of a smile graced his lips as he shook his head in amusement. He had better feed me soon.

As if hearing my thoughts, just then, like a whisper of movement, I caught sight of it—a flash of fur darting between the trees. My heart leaped in excitement as I nudged Logan, pointing in the direction of our quarry.

With practiced precision, Logan adjusted the snare we'd set earlier, his movements fluid and silent. I watched in awe as he positioned it just so, ensuring that our trap was perfectly placed to ensnare the unsuspecting rabbit.

Time seemed to stand still as we waited, our breaths shallow and quiet, the tension palpable in the air. I could feel the adrenaline coursing through my veins, heightening my senses as we prepared to strike.

And then, in a heartbeat, it happened—the rabbit emerged from its hiding place, drawn by the scent of food we left as bait. My heart raced as I watched it draw nearer, its movements cautious yet determined.

With a quick glance at Logan, we shared a silent understanding. This was our moment.

The rabbit stepped into the trap, and there was a soft click as the snare sprang shut, capturing our prey in an instant. A surge of triumph rushed through me as I watched Logan retrieve the rabbit, his hands deft and sure as he checked the trap.

"Yay!" I said as I watched him bring it back; even if I couldn't bring myself to think about why such a beautiful creature had to die, my stomach was thinking differently.

"Come on, let's go."

I nodded and started to follow Logan; we moved through the forest together, silently witnessing the beauty that surrounded us. I stopped when I caught sight of a squirrel quietly napping in one of the trees. I became transfixed.

"Take the shot then." Logan's voice pierced my thoughts, and I nodded again, happy that he had figured out what I wanted.

The sky was ablaze with a riot of colors, and it was so perfect that I found myself completely entranced by the untouched magnificence of the wilderness. With my camera clasped firmly in my hands, I took a few shots.

I looked back at him, my lower lip jutting out in a pout, and he sighed before smiling. "Go ahead, I knew you wouldn't stop soon."

I wondered how he knew so many things; over the past two weeks, we'd both arrived at some sort of conclusion without talking about it. We focused on paying attention to each other's needs and talking more; slowly, we forged a tentative bond.

Despite our differences, we found strength and comfort in each other's company and a shared determination to survive. Going out to hunt and gather firewood together had become a norm; while he hunted and collected wood, I usually worked on my photography.

We slowly learned to rely on each other and develop mutual respect and understanding. Without needing to worry about the what-ifs and arguments, I was able to focus more on honing my skills.

I found myself drawn to the raw and untamed beauty of the wilderness, discovering a newfound sense of freedom and purpose. Even though my leg continued to heal slowly, and I made sure to not hurt it anymore, neither of us spoke about when I would leave.

It was like a sacred discussion that we kept out of the conversation until we could no longer shove it aside. As I became one with my camera, I shook my head to dispel the thoughts.

I focused instead on how the air was alive with the symphony of nature, the melodious chirping of birds and the rustle of leaves underfoot, all creating a harmonious backdrop to my focus.

Shafts of golden light filtered through the dense foliage, casting intricate patterns on the forest floor, and illuminating hidden corners with a soft, ethereal glow. Every click of the shutter felt like a moment frozen in time, a fleeting glimpse of the world's raw and unfiltered beauty captured through the lens of my camera.

As I wandered deeper into the heart of the forest, my senses were overwhelmed by the sheer abundance of life that surrounded me. The earthy scent of pine needles mingled with the sweet perfume of wildflowers, filling the air with a heady fragrance that stirred something primal within me.

In the distance, I could sense Logan's presence. His quiet watchfulness was a reassuring presence in the vast expanse of nature. I knew I could let go and trust him to protect me. With each photograph I took, I felt a profound sense of connection to the world around me, a deepening appreciation for the intricate beauty that existed in every leaf, every blade of grass.

I forgot I was hungry until Logan joined me, his footsteps a soft whisper against the forest floor. Together, we pored over the images, each one a masterpiece of light and shadow, texture and color.

"The weather is so perfect; I need to show you this," he said as he massaged my shoulder blades. "I've been meaning to keep it to myself, but I think you will appreciate it more."

"Really?" I was getting excited since I knew Logan was a man of his word; if he said something was worth it, then it was.

"Come on, I might even give you a massage when we get there." He nudged and turned on his heels, leaving me to follow him.

Excitement gave a spring to my steps as Logan led me through the winding paths, each step bringing us closer to the hidden gem he had promised to show me. I could feel the thrill building within me, a sense of anticipation tinged with wonder as we ventured deeper into the heart of the wilderness, and I noted it was a path we'd never taken.

As we rounded a bend in the trail, a soft gasp escaped my lips as a lake came into view, nestled amid a grove of towering trees. The water shimmered like liquid silver in the dappled sunlight, its surface reflecting the golden hues of the surrounding foliage in a breathtaking display of natural beauty.

I stood transfixed on the shoreline, my gaze tracing the gentle ripples that danced across the surface of the lake. The air was alive with the sound of birdsong and the soft murmur of water cascading over rocks; it filled me with a sense of peace and serenity.

Logan watched me with a smile, his eyes crinkling at the corners as he took in my awe-inspired expression. Without a word, he reached out a hand, his fingers intertwining with mine as he led me closer to the water's edge.

"See? I knew you would like it."

"I love it! I will forgive you for not bringing me sooner," I said as we walked along the shore and the cool breeze stirred the tendrils of hair around my face as we drank in the beauty of our surroundings.

Each step brought us closer to the heart of the lake where the water stretched out before us like a vast, untamed canvas waiting to be explored. I dropped my camera, needing to soak in the beauty first and think about the best angle to take pictures.

We reached the water's edge, and I knelt down to dip my fingers into the crystal-clear liquid, feeling its cool embrace against my skin. The lake seemed to pulse with life, a living entity that beckoned me to immerse myself in its depths and lose myself in its tranquil embrace.

"Thank you, Logan," I said excitedly as I looked back again at the lake, an idea slowly filling my head. "I want to skinny dip."

"Really?" Logan asked in surprise, but I was already hiking the shirt I wore, another of his, over my head and stepping out of my underwear.

"Fuck, woman, you know how to push me to the edge," Logan drawled as his gaze trailed over my body. "I think I should give you the message before you go in; we need to warm up your blood. The lake is colder than it looks."

He stepped closer; the warmth of his touch against my skin sent a shiver down my spine, igniting a fire within me that I couldn't contain. My body responded eagerly to his caress, my skin flushing with desire as his hands roamed over me.

His fingers trailed up from my belly to the sides of my breasts; I couldn't help but arch toward him, craving his touch on my aching buds. But he teased me, keeping his distance from my nipples as I squirmed beneath him, yearning for more.

Whether it was his thoughtfulness when it came to me, just his masterful touch, or a combination of both, my skin throbbed and my nipples stood erect. I could feel the insides of my thighs becoming soaked, and I wanted him to touch me there.

He slowly guided me so I was sitting on the fine sand beside the lake before he pushed me down, the sand warming my back nicely as his fingers walked up my shoulders; he dug them in with force like he would knead dough.

From my shoulders, he moved down my arms, squeezing and rubbing my biceps and then pressing his fingers into my palms. I relaxed my muscles, releasing my tension. Something inside me unfurled and stretched out, like a cat basking in the sun.

He was still fully dressed, but his muscles stood out firm and well-defined; my eyes trailed down to where I could see the slight bulge against his pants, and I could tell he was partially erect.

"Would you like me to go down further and massage your pussy?" he said in a husky voice, and I could see the bulge increase.

It sounded like a wonderful idea; no one had ever massaged my pussy before. "Absolutely," I gushed. My pussy was drenched in anticipation. I moaned, pushing myself against him. Sensations rushed over me as he bent to kiss my pussy.

"You're so beautiful down here, so much that it drives me insane," he whispered into my folds.

His words shot through my body, sending tingles all the way to my fingertips and toes. Delicately, he probed around the lips, licking up one side and then down the other. I moaned and pushed forward, seeking more sensation as the sand rubbed against my back and ass, giving a whole different sensation.

Teasingly, Logan pulled back and traced his finger up and down my drenched slit again, making me wetter. Then he plunged his tongue back in, slurping up my juices. I'd come to realize that he always took pleasure in my pleasure.

I relaxed fully and focused on my breathing as he licked and probed me, settling into a steady rhythm. My thighs trembled like I was in a spasm when he removed his tongue, slid a finger inside me, and began stroking it in and out.

"You taste so good," he moaned with a deep baritone sound that vibrated through my pussy and sent a twinge shooting up my spine.

Energy rushed through me, my body floated, and I held a fistful of sand in my hands. I wanted him to put in a second finger and fill me up, and he did without me having to say a thing.

My orgasm was building; the sensation and intensity was so strong that I could no longer moan. When he reached up with his free hand and flicked my left nipple, a river exploded from me, drenching between my thighs, and seeping out.

Logan was there to catch the juices, his tongue lapping them up. He swallowed every last drop, and that was the final nudge to send me completely over the edge. The explosion blew hot shards of sensation into every cell, and my mind faded to black from the multiple orgasms.

For a timeless stretch, I was enveloped in a state of serene bliss, where thoughts ceased to form, and I simply surrendered to the gentle undulations of ecstasy. Gradually, the haze in my mind lifted, and I emerged from the dissipating fog.

At last, I blinked open my eyes to the familiar sight of trees surrounding us. The melodious chorus of birdsong resumed, filling the air with its harmonious cadence. Logan knelt before me on the sand, his countenance suffused with a serene and contented expression.

"What about you?" I asked, stroking his rock-hard dick with my foot.

He smiled and kissed me, getting up from the sand. "Today was about you."

"Let me make you feel good." I reached out, but he stepped away.

"Get into the lake then and fill my gaze."

I nodded; I could do that much.

Much later, I emerged from the serene waters of the lake after bidding from Logan; I couldn't resist for much longer, especially since the hunger was back at its fullest. I allowed him to help me dress.

"If you had remained longer in the lake, you could have gotten a cold," Logan chided after my shirt was in place and he turned around to start walking in the direction of the cabin.

I had no sooner taken a few steps when a sudden weakness gripped me like invisible hands tightening around my chest. It was as if the cool embrace of the water had drained me of every ounce of strength, leaving me trembling and unsteady on my feet.

The world around me began to blur and sway, each step feeling like a monumental effort as I struggled to keep pace with Logan. My muscles screamed in protest, my breaths coming in ragged gasps as I fought against the overwhelming urge to collapse.

The sounds of the forest grew distant and muffled as if I were submerged underwater; the gentle rustle of leaves and the distant calls of birds faded into an eerie silence. My vision dimmed at the edges, a creeping darkness encroaching upon my consciousness.

I reached out for Logan, my fingers trembling as they brushed against his arm, seeking support in the midst of my faltering strength. But even his solid presence couldn't hold back the tide of weakness that threatened to engulf me.

With a soft moan, I felt my knees buckle beneath me, my body sinking toward the forest floor as if pulled by invisible strings. I fought against the darkness, willing myself to stay conscious, but it was a futile effort.

And then, with a final, whispered breath, I succumbed to the darkness, my world fading to black as unconsciousness claimed me in its embrace.

13

LOGAN

I couldn't believe how excited she was about the lake, and it almost made me feel bad for hiding and keeping it all to myself. I'd always opted to get water for her every morning rather than allow her to visit the lake by herself.

I told myself it was my way of protecting myself against the time when she'd leave. I couldn't bear to have every part of the forest and my cabin reminding me of her. Over the past two weeks, I'd come to the conclusion that I would miss her terribly by the time she left; she'd come to mean so much more to me than I cared to admit.

But looking at her being so giddy and excited made me realize it would have been my loss if she hadn't seen the lake. I loved seeing her free and excited, almost as much as I loved seeing her naked and beneath me.

My mood was lifted, and the forest seemed to hum with life around me. Every rustle and chirp was a testament to the vibrant ecosystem thriving in its depths. But suddenly, as if a switch had been flipped, the cacophony of sounds abruptly ceased, replaced by an eerie silence that sent shivers down my spine.

My heart leaped into my throat as I whirled around, my senses on high alert, only to be met with the heart-stopping sight of Elena crumpling to the ground behind me. Time seemed to slow to a crawl as panic surged through my veins, my mind struggling to process the sight before me.

Abandoning all thoughts of the rabbit I had caught before, I threw it to the side and sprinted to Elena, my pulse thundering in my ears as I dropped to my knees beside her.

"Elena!" I cried out, my voice raw with fear as I gently cradled her limp form in my arms.

Her skin felt unnaturally cold against mine, her features pale and drawn as she lay unmoving in my embrace. My hands shook as I brushed a stray strand of hair from her face, my mind racing with a million worst-case scenarios.

What had caused her to collapse so suddenly? Was she injured? Sick? The questions swirled in my mind like a tempest, each one more terrifying than the last as I struggled to make sense of the situation.

I held her fragile form in my arms and gazed down at her still body. A fierce determination rose within me; I would do whatever it took to ensure her safety, even if it meant facing the darkest depths of the wilderness alone.

As I lifted Elena's unconscious body into my arms, a wave of dizziness washed over me, threatening to send me toppling to the forest floor alongside her. But I gritted my teeth against the nausea, my muscles straining with the effort as I staggered back toward the cabin.

Every step felt like a battle against the weight of the world itself. The forest seemed to close around us, its ancient trees whispering secrets that I was too terrified to hear. With every step, the weight of her limp form felt heavier, even though I knew she was very light.

But at the moment, she was pressing down on me like a burden I could scarcely bear. I refused to falter, my mind consumed by a single, desperate thought: I had to get her to the cabin safely, no matter the cost.

As we trudged through the wilderness, my thoughts spiraled into a whirlwind of fear and uncertainty. What if she didn't wake up? What if she was gravely ill, her life hanging in the balance? The thought sent a chill down my spine, filling me with a bone-deep dread that threatened to consume me whole.

But even as my mind raced with worst-case scenarios, another, darker thought lurked at the edges of my consciousness; what if this was just the beginning? What if Elena's collapse was just the first sign of a looming catastrophe, a harbinger of the same fate that had befallen so many others in my life?

The thought was like a knife twisting in my gut, filling me with a sickening sense of inevitability. It was as if my past had come back to haunt me once more, reminding me of the cruel twist of fate that seemed to follow me wherever I went.

Finally, we reached the cabin, a sanctuary in the heart of the wilderness. As I pushed open the door and laid Elena down on the bed, a fierce determination rose within me. I refused to let history repeat itself. I would do whatever it took to protect her, to keep her safe from my curse.

As I laid Elena down on the bed, a rush of panic flooded through me, mingled with a bone-deep exhaustion that threatened to pull me under. With trembling hands, I brushed a lock of hair from her face, my heart aching with a fierce, protective love.

I moved her across the bed, making sure she was comfortable and secure. My hands moved with practiced care, tucking the blankets around her form, and ensuring she was shielded from the chill that had suddenly permeated the air and seeped through the cabin walls.

As I looked down at her still figure, a pang of worry tightened its grip around my heart. She seemed so fragile, so vulnerable in this moment of unconsciousness. But I refused to let fear paralyze me. Instead, I focused on what I could do to help her, ease her discomfort, and ensure her well-being.

I fetched a damp cloth from the basin of water nearby and gently dabbed it against her forehead, wondering if it would help, especially with the coolness that lingered on her skin. With each stroke, I whispered words of reassurance, hoping that somehow she could sense my presence and find comfort in it.

I checked her pulse, my fingers pressing gently against the delicate skin of her wrist as I monitored the steady rhythm of her heartbeat. It was a small comfort, knowing that she was still alive, still fighting even in her unconscious state.

Throughout the day, I remained by her side, tending to her needs as best as I could. I kept a watchful eye on her breathing, adjusting the blankets when she stirred restlessly and murmured soothing words into the silence of the cabin.

As night fell, the moonlight filtered through the window and cast a soft glow over her sleeping form. I found a sense of purpose in caring for her even though I was almost running mad with impatience.

It was a simple act but one filled with meaning and significance. As I watched over her, I vowed to do whatever it took to ensure her safety and well-being, no matter the cost.

I sat beside Elena's still form, and a solemn vow took shape in the depths of my soul. I refused to let fate dictate our future or to resign myself to the cruel whims of chance. If there was one thing I could control in this chaotic world, it was my determination to keep her safe.

I was being selfish by keeping her with me, and this was just fate's way of reminding me about what would happen if I insisted on doing so, the same thing that had happened to everyone I kept by my side and would happen to anyone I intended to keep there.

I reaffirmed my resolve. If Elena woke up, if she regained consciousness and looked into my eyes once more, I would let her go. I wouldn't mind how painful and lonely I would be after she left; what mattered would be me loving her enough to let her go, to protect her.

It wasn't an easy decision, and the weight of it pressed down on me like a burden too heavy to bear. But I knew deep down that it was the only choice I could make, the only way to ensure that she would be spared from the dangers that lurked around me.

And so, as the hours stretched on and the flickering light of the cabin lantern cast long shadows across the room, I made a silent promise to myself and to Elena. No matter how much it pained me, no matter how much my heart longed to hold onto her, I would set her free.

I was wondering what I could do to make her wake up; it felt dangerous for her to remain unconscious for so long, especially since she hadn't shown any signs of illness before. I stripped her, checking her all over for wounds I might have missed that could have gotten infected, but there were none.

I checked on her leg, fearing she was suffering from some kind of reaction, but it was all fine. I got to my feet and started to pace around the cabin like a wounded animal, wondering how to get back at fate for being so cruel and unforgiving.

I would never forgive myself if anything happened to her.

"Uhg…" A moaning sound echoed throughout the room as Elena stirred awake in the middle of the night.

"Elena?" I whisper-yelled as a surge of relief flooded through me like a tidal wave. It was as though a heavy weight had been lifted from my shoulders, replaced by a newfound sense of hope and reassurance.

Without a second thought, I reached out and enveloped her in my arms, drawing her close to me with a fierce sense of protectiveness. Her presence against my chest felt like a lifeline, anchoring me to the reality of the moment.

I held her close, afraid she might slip away again if I let go. Her warmth pressed against me; her steady heartbeat was a comforting rhythm against my chest.

In the soft glow of the moonlight filtering through the window, I gazed down at her, taking in every detail of her face illuminated by its gentle light. There was a vulnerability in her eyes, a rawness that spoke of the trials she had faced and the strength she had shown in overcoming them.

"What happened?" she groaned, her voice sounding muffled against my chest. She looked up at me, her eyes searching mine as if seeking some unspoken answer.

"You fainted," I murmured.

"My body feels weird but rested," she murmured again. I brushed a stray strand of hair from her face, my fingers lingering against her cheek as I drank in the sight of her.

"You've been asleep since this afternoon," I explained. "I was afraid you wouldn't wake up; I didn't know what to do."

"I don't know what happened, either." Her words made my throat tighten up so that I couldn't swallow. She couldn't even begin to imagine just how much she had come to mean to me.

"Don't scare me like that again," I chided, still holding her tightly to me.

"I didn't want to."

I realized something else at that moment; I loved her. It was a revelation that both frightened and exhilarated me, stirring emotions within me that I had long kept buried deep beneath the surface.

Without a word, I leaned down and pressed my lips to hers, a gentle caress that spoke volumes of the feelings swirling between us. It was a kiss filled with tenderness and longing, a silent promise of the bond that had formed between us in the quiet moments of the night.

I loved her! It kept ricocheting in my head.

14

ELENA

It was getting harder to breathe as Logan held me tightly in his arms. It had been a little over twenty minutes, and I could still feel the tension radiating from his body, his fear palpable against my skin; it was almost like he had no intention of letting go.

But I didn't mind; in fact, I welcomed his embrace, understanding that it was his way of seeking comfort since I knew I must have scared him. His hold was almost too tight; his arms wrapped around me with a desperate urgency that spoke volumes about his emotions.

Yet, I didn't pull away. Instead, I leaned into him, allowing myself to be engulfed by his warmth and strength. In the stillness of the cabin, with only the sound of our breathing filling the air, I closed my eyes and let myself relax in his embrace.

His scent, a mixture of pine, leather, and nature, surrounded me, cocooning me in a sense of safety and security that I hadn't felt in a long time. His heartbeat echoed in my ears, and I felt a wave of tenderness wash over me, a deep appreciation for the man who held me so fiercely.

"You must have fainted because you didn't eat all day," Logan said against my ear. "I left the rabbit back at the lake, but I'm sure it would be eaten by now. I'll just make some soup for us instead."

"Thank you, Logan." He probably didn't know how much I appreciated him.

"Does anywhere hurt?" he asked as he pulled back and looked me all over.

It was weird that, aside from being tired, despite sleeping the majority of the day away, having mild abdominal pain, and feeling warm to the touch, I felt fine otherwise. So, why did I faint?

"No, nothing hurts. At least nothing that a warm soup wouldn't chase away." I flashed him a reassuring smile.

He nodded, "I had better get to it then." I watched him go; his expression appeared shrunk, and his gait a little unsteady. It made me feel bad that I did that to him.

I felt a wave of nausea wash over me as the door closed behind him; it brought my thoughts back to myself, and my mind raced with concern and uncertainty. What could possibly be causing this sudden bout of sickness and fainting?

As far as I knew, I'd always been healthy and never suffered from a fainting spell. Was it something I ate, or perhaps a reaction to the change in the environment after weeks of being out in the wilderness?

I tried to dismiss the idea that my body was protesting against my new surroundings. After all, I had never felt better than I did out here in nature, surrounded by the trees and the fresh air. It had been a welcome escape from the stresses of city life, and I had relished every moment of it.

But still, the nagging worry persisted. Could it be something more serious? Was I coming down with an illness, or worse, was it a sign of something else entirely?

I shook my head, trying to clear away the doubts and fears that threatened to overwhelm me. I couldn't afford to panic, not when there were so many unknowns. Instead, I focused on taking deep breaths and calming my racing heart.

Whatever the cause of my sudden sickness, I knew one thing for certain: I needed to take care of myself and listen to what my body was trying to tell me. Only then could I hope to find some answers and ease the unease that gnawed at my mind.

Hold on. Was my period about to show up? Had I been eating enough? I tried to remember the last time I felt this way, but my memory was all fuzzy. Then, I got worried. What if it was something serious? Was I not eating right, and my body rebelling? Maybe Logan was right.

I started counting days, trying to figure out what was up with my body. Had I skipped too many meals lately? Was I not taking care of myself like I should? But then, it hit me. I remembered the day Logan saved me. I was ovulating; the reminder from my tracking app had pinged before I left the phone behind that day.

Now, I remember why I was feeling a bit off at that time, why I couldn't shake the weird, tingly sensation when Logan touched me. It was like my body was buzzing with energy, but I couldn't figure out why then.

That familiar twinge, that extra bit of warmth spreading through me. It was like a switch had been flipped, and suddenly, I was feeling all sorts of things. It would definitely explain why I found it difficult to resist him.

It was because my body was on high alert and ready to be taken. My mind drifted back to the way Logan's eyes sparkled in the sunlight and how his smile made my heart skip a beat. And then there was this other feeling, this strong ache that seemed to radiate from somewhere deep inside me.

It was like a hunger, but not for food. My thoughts kept drifting to Logan, to the way he looked at me, the way he touched me. It was like my body was screaming at me, telling me to do something, but I didn't know what. It must have been because I was ovulating.

I shot to my feet. My period usually came between ten to thirteen days after ovulating, and I'd spent close to a month with Logan; I had yet to get my period. My hands flew to my mouth in shock as the realization washed over me like a tidal wave.

Pregnant?

It seemed impossible, yet the signs were unmistakable; we'd been having sex without protection. How could I have been so careless? I had totally forgotten about my pills, too. My hands came down to rest on my belly. Now what?

The weight of the revelation settled heavily on my shoulders, filling me with a tumult of conflicting emotions. Fear gripped me like a vice, squeezing the air from my lungs and leaving me gasping for breath.

The thought of bringing a new life into the world filled me with a deep sense of unease. Could I handle the responsibilities of parenthood amid our wilderness existence? What would Logan say? How would he react to the news?

Every possible scenario played out in my mind, each one accompanied by a fresh wave of anxiety. Dread gnawed at my insides, twisting my stomach into knots as I contemplated the uncertain future that lay ahead.

Taking a shaky breath, I struggled to steady my racing thoughts. There was no room for me to panic. I knew I had to be strong, but the weight of the unknown bore down on me with crushing force, leaving me feeling overwhelmed and uncertain about how things would proceed.

But first thing, I needed to tell Logan.

I paced back and forth in the small cabin for a minute, my heart pounding in my chest like a drumbeat of impending doom. Panic clawed at the edges of my mind, threatening to consume me whole.

How could I tell him? How would he react? Would he be angry? Scared? Overwhelmed? We were not even an item, officially, and now this was happening? I couldn't bear the thought of disappointing him or adding to his burdens.

I stilled my thoughts, reminding myself that we'd made the baby together and I shouldn't be scared of what he would think.

The thought made me step outside; I knew I couldn't keep it to myself for a minute longer. He was right there, cutting vegetables and spring onions into the pot over the open fire.

"You must be hungry; I'll soon be done," he said without looking up.

I didn't reply but resumed my pacing, the weight of my revelation pressing down on me like a leaden cloak. It was the right time to tell him, but the words were caught in my throat, choking me. What if he reacted badly? What if he blamed me for our predicament?

I approached him, and my steps faltered, my resolve waning with each passing moment. Logan glanced up from his cooking, concern etched on his features as he noticed my distress.

"Hey, Elena, what's wrong?" he asked, his voice gentle but tinged with worry.

I opened my mouth to speak, but no words came out. Panic surged through me, constricting my chest, and stealing my breath. Logan set aside his cooking utensils and stepped closer, his eyes searching mine for answers.

"Hey, talk to me. What's going on?" he urged, his hand reaching out to touch my arm.

I flinched at his touch, my anxiety reaching a fever pitch as I struggled to find the courage to speak. With a shaky breath, I finally blurted out the words that had been weighing heavily on my mind.

"I have something to tell you," I started, glancing up to gauge his mood.

"Okay, sit here. Are you hurting somewhere?"

"I... I think I might be pregnant," I blurted, my voice barely above a whisper.

Logan's expression shifted from concern to shock, his features frozen in disbelief for a moment before registering the gravity of my words. He took a step back, his eyes widening as he processed the news.

"Pregnant?" he repeated, his voice barely more than a hoarse whisper.

I nodded, unable to meet his gaze as a fresh wave of fear washed over me. The silence stretched between us, heavy with unspoken questions and unvoiced fears.

The weight of my words hung in the air, a palpable tension that seemed to stretch on endlessly. As I watched Logan's reaction unfold before me, I couldn't help but feel a sense of apprehension mingled with the raw intensity of my emotions.

I didn't know what I wanted or expected from him, but it wasn't the indifference that settled across his features or his return back to cooking, continuing to stir the soup as though I hadn't told him something that would change our lives, well at least mine.

It was far-fetched to expect him to jump for joy or carry me around in ecstasy; I would be lying if I said I didn't know that he had his life planned out in the wilderness. Besides, excitement was the furthest thing from my mind.

Still, any reaction would have been better aside from that. At that moment, everything felt magnified, as if the world had suddenly shifted on its axis, leaving me suspended in a state of uncertainty.

The revelation of my possible pregnancy definitely cast a new light on our relationship and would probably illuminate the depths of our connection in ways I had never anticipated.

For me, it was a moment of reckoning, a stark realization of the profound impact this could have on our lives. Motherhood loomed on the horizon, a daunting prospect that filled me with equal parts fear and wonder. Would I be ready for such a responsibility? Could I handle the challenges that lay ahead?

I turned around and walked back into the cabin, my appetite gone, and I was left wondering about what I would do if Logan didn't want to be a part of the baby's life.

15

LOGAN

I realized I had been foolish.

I shouldn't have made a bet with fate; I shouldn't have assumed I was powerful and could somehow change fate when I was, in fact, powerless. Maybe if I wasn't so full of myself, things wouldn't have spiraled out of control.

It had begun with the realization that I was wholly and fully in love with her, then to grappling with the fact that I would have to send her away whether I wanted to or not, and now she was pregnant and carrying my baby.

A child born from my semen, carrying my genes and DNA, who would probably have Elena's eyes and resemble her, or who was supposed to be a mini-me after birth; but I couldn't even bring myself to feel excited or be happy.

It had been six whole days since the fainting episode and her telling me the news; there had been no exchange of words between us, and the news had changed everything for us.

While we remained silent and were locked in our own world, the pregnancy slowly became real. She started to experience the first bouts of morning sickness; nothing would stay down except ginger tea and soup, and while I held her hair and rubbed her back, I always found myself tongue-tied.

This morning she had been too weak to even stand after vomiting throughout the early hours, so I chose to wipe her down. As I gazed down at Elena's body, my eyes were drawn to the subtle but unmistakable changes that pregnancy had already begun to bring about.

It was her breasts that first captured my attention, their once familiar curves now accentuated by a newfound fullness and roundness. They seemed to have swelled with the promise of a new life, the soft contours now more pronounced.

Her tummy, too, showed subtle signs of the growing life within. A gentle swell was beginning to form, barely perceptible but unmistakable to my eyes. It was a testament to the miracle unfolding within her, a silent announcement of the new journey we were embarking upon together.

As I took in these changes, a mixture of emotions washed over me. There was awe at the sheer miracle of life's wonder and the incredible changes taking place before my eyes. But there was also a sense of protectiveness, a fierce determination to shield Elena and our unborn child from harm.

Still, I couldn't help but fear. It was one thing when it was just us both; I was willing to be selfless and let her go just to protect her. She's amazing, and anyone would be happy to find a woman like her. I knew she would heal.

Now that I knew she was pregnant and I was slowly seeing her body change; I wasn't selfless enough to let them go. I wasn't selfless enough to not want to be a part of their lives and at least have a chance at happiness.

Despite the flickers of fear and doubt that danced at the edges of my mind, I couldn't deny the swell of emotion that surged within me at the thought of the child Elena carried. It was a bittersweet realization, tinged with the lingering shadows of my past and the uncertainty of our future.

But I feared they would bear the consequences for my selfishness. Part of me couldn't shake the nagging worry that my curse would somehow be passed on to our child, that the misfortunes of my past would haunt the innocent life growing within Elena's womb.

Even as that fear gnawed at me, another part was filled with a fierce determination to protect and nurture both Elena and our unborn baby. I wanted to shield them from harm, to wrap them in a cocoon of love and safety that would keep the darkness at bay.

I longed to embrace the joy and happiness that should have accompanied the news of impending parenthood, but I found myself unable to fully let go of my fears and insecurities.

Was it selfish of me to want this child, knowing what was going to tag along with it? Shouldn't I be more concerned with protecting Elena and our baby from the uncertainties of my past? These questions haunted me, casting a shadow over what should have been a moment of celebration.

However, one thing remained clear. I wanted this child, this tangible symbol of the love that Elena and I shared. But I also couldn't bring myself to feel joy and happiness when I knew I was being selfish.

Maybe that was why I told myself it was okay to go off after her morning sickness so I could find a semblance of peace amidst the turmoil of my thoughts. Over the past six days, the routine of preparing for the day ahead became my refuge, a way to distract myself from the weight of responsibility that now rested heavily on my shoulders.

I always busied myself with gathering necessities and stocking up on food every time I couldn't shake the feeling of unease that gnawed at the edges of my consciousness. I would cook both breakfast and lunch and leave something light for her to eat for dinner.

The decision to distance myself from Elena weighed heavily on my heart, but it felt like the only way to shield her from the storm brewing within me. I couldn't bear to see the worry in her eyes or the uncertainty that clouded her expression whenever she looked at me.

It was a painful reminder of the burden I carried, the fear that my presence would only bring harm to her and our unborn child. And so, I would always slip away before she woke from her nap in the evening, leaving only a note to let her know I had been there.

It was a feeble attempt to reassure her that I still cared, and that my absence was not a rejection but a misguided attempt to protect her from the darkness that lurked within me.

But with each passing day, the distance between us grew, a silent chasm widening with each unspoken word and missed opportunity for connection. As I watched her sleeping form each night, a pang of regret always pierced my heart, a reminder of the love I longed to express but dared not show.

I knew I was being selfish and that my actions only served to deepen the divide between us. But I couldn't find the words to bridge the gap, couldn't bring myself to open up and share the weight of my fears and insecurities.

So, I retreated into the shadows, a silent sentinel keeping watch over the woman I loved from a distance, hoping against hope that she would forgive me for my silence and understand the depth of my devotion, even as I struggled to find the courage to show it.

The routine became simple; I would be gone once she slept after vomiting in the morning and would only return when I was certain she was asleep at night.

Each night, I would watch Elena lay asleep on the bed, her breathing slow and steady. I longed to hold her in my arms, to feel the warmth of her body pressed against mine, to lose myself in the heat of passion that had once consumed us both.

But even as the desire burned hot in my veins, I knew that giving in to it would only lead to heartache and regret. So, I would lay there on the floor with the flickering firelight keeping my company, my fists clenched in frustration, while my heart was heavy with longing.

I knew that I had to stay strong, that I had to resist the urge to reach out to her, no matter how much it pained me to do so. I couldn't bear to risk causing her any more pain than I already had.

The night would wear on, and sleep would continue to elude me. The ache in my chest always grew more pronounced, a constant reminder of the love I dared not acknowledge and the desire I dared not act upon.

I would lay awake in the darkness, tormented by thoughts of what could have been; I knew that I would carry this burden with me for as long as I drew breath.

Tonight was no different.

The moon hung high in the night sky, casting its pale glow over the quiet wilderness surrounding the cabin. As I approached the familiar wooden structure, a sense of apprehension gripped me, tightening like a vice around my chest. I hesitated at the threshold, my hand hovering over the door handle, uncertainty holding me back.

In the stillness of the night, the only sound was the soft rustle of leaves in the breeze and the distant call of a nocturnal bird. Yet, despite the tranquil exterior, a tempest of conflicting emotions threatened to consume my resolve.

Part of me longed to step inside, to seek solace in the warmth of the fire and the comfort of Elena's presence. But another part hesitated, weighed down by the fear of facing the truth that awaited me within those walls.

With a heavy sigh, I finally pushed open the door and stepped inside, the familiar scent of wood smoke and pine greeting me like an old friend. The fire crackled in the hearth, casting flickering shadows across the room and bathing everything in a soft, golden light.

Elena lay asleep on the makeshift bed, her form outlined by the gentle glow of the fire. For a moment, I simply stood there, drinking in the sight of her, the rise and fall of her chest as she breathed, the peaceful expression on her face that contrasted with the confusion in my own heart.

I moved closer, and a wave of guilt washed over me, threatening to drown me in its icy depths. I had stayed away too long and allowed my fears to drive a wedge between us that now seemed insurmountable. And though I longed to reach out to her, to bridge the gap that had grown between us, I couldn't shake the feeling of unworthiness that gnawed at my soul.

With a heavy heart, I sank down onto the edge of the bed, my gaze fixed on Elena's sleeping form. How could I explain the reasons for my absence, the doubts and fears that plagued me with each passing day? How could I make her understand the depth of my love when I struggled to comprehend it myself?

Just as I was about to get up and move to the floor, convinced that she was lost in the depths of sleep, she stirred, her movements slow and deliberate. With a soft rustle of sheets, she opened her eyes and gazed at me directly, her eyes glinting in the faint moonlight that filtered through the window.

For a moment, we simply gazed at each other in silence. And then, in a voice barely above a whisper, she spoke.

"I'll be returning home tomorrow," she said, her words tinged with resignation. "It's time for me to go back.

Her words hit me like a thunderbolt, shattering the cacophony of voices in my head. Leaving only the reality of her impending departure that crashed down on me with crushing force, leaving me reeling in its wake.

A sudden clarity washed over me like a wave crashing against the shore. The pieces of the puzzle clicked into place; she had been patient enough, and she wouldn't wait forever for me to get my life on track.

So, she was leaving.

She was giving in to my efforts to distance myself, to keep my emotions in check. But the thought of her leaving filled me with a sense of panic and dread I couldn't quite explain. It was as if a part of me had come alive in her presence, a part I had tried so desperately to bury beneath layers of stoicism and self-denial.

Taking a deep breath to steady my nerves, I reached out to touch her cheek, the warmth of her skin sending a jolt of electricity coursing through my veins. "Why?" I asked, my voice barely a whisper in the stillness of the night.

Elena met my gaze with a mixture of sadness and resolve, her eyes shimmering with unshed tears. "I have to," she replied softly, her words echoing in the quiet of the room. "It's time for me to go back home, to face the reality I've been running from for so long."

She didn't wait for me to reply; instead, she turned around and ignored my existence. Those few words were the first we'd said to each other all week.

16

ELENA

I was in love with Logan, and it had just taken me a while to realize it.

Ever since the realization, I'd been on an emotional rollercoaster, not only because the man I'd fallen in love with wasn't showing any inclination to reciprocate but also because he obviously wasn't happy with the news that I was careless enough to get pregnant.

It definitely didn't help matters that the pregnancy symptoms were becoming more severe, and the serenity of the forest and the smell of nature that had appealed to me when I'd first arrived was starting to repulse me.

After the day I told Logan the news, he didn't give any sort of reaction. First, I'd been hurt, bewildered, and lonely. Then I sat down and tried to analyze the situation, considering that perhaps there was something I was overlooking. But nothing surfaced in my head.

I told myself to give him space and that he would surely come around, but days passed until it was an entire week, and it became apparent to me that it was my wishful thinking; Logan wasn't going to come around.

I was furious and told myself that it didn't matter where he stood, neither did I give a damn about him.

But I overlooked the fact that lying to myself wasn't my forte, and I sucked at it. So, while the anger held me up, it helped me through the morning sickness and to hold my tongue whenever he chose to hold my hair, cook for me, and make me comfortable while remaining stubbornly silent.

Deep down, I still cared. I thought about everything until I realized I truly loved him, which was why I felt so devastated. I loved him enough to swallow my pride and wait until he was back from the woods and to tell him I would finally be leaving.

I hoped it would make him rethink; maybe he would finally break down and tell me what the problem was, maybe he would see the light and realize how important I was to him, and maybe he would tell me he wanted the baby very much.

But all he asked was, "Why?" So I turned and slept with my back to him.

It was morning now, and so far, there had been nothing else he'd said. And I was starting to realize how much I didn't matter to him and that he was never going to say what I wanted to hear.

Once I left the woods, it would be over, and I'd probably never see him again. I would keep my feelings to myself and go away silently. I didn't think it would make any difference if I chose to declare my love for him loudly; I'd probably end up chasing him further into his shell.

I believed an entire week was enough to get an answer from him, and I was done waiting. I didn't want to believe his true response was taking off every day and leaving me to my devices.

Nor did I want to believe that all I deserved and would get from him despite everything we shared would be "why?" It was so ludicrous that I could feel the anger bubbling up inside of me, but I calmed myself intentionally. It wouldn't do any good for the baby.

While I couldn't force him to talk to me and tell me his decision, it was also true that he couldn't hold me back from leaving. There was no reason for me to sit around and wait for him forever.

I would make the moves from my own end, especially since he had asked me to leave once my leg was done healing. I would chalk it up to him not having enough decency to say that he wanted me to stay.

My legs were healed enough to walk with a subtle limp, and in a week or two, I would be fine. So, there was nothing else stopping me from leaving.

I continued to pretend to sleep for a minute longer, my arms wrapped protectively around where my baby was growing. My decision was simple; I would keep the baby and care for it all alone.

Money wasn't a problem; I had enough funds to support both of us and my family to fall back on in case I needed more. I could also count on my father and mother for emotional support. It didn't get any better than that.

He wanted space? That's why he always left in the morning and returned late into the night. Well, he'd have his cabin back and the entire woods all to himself.

I got up from the bed with a groan as a wave of nausea bubbled up; I looked down and realized I was foolish for pretending to be asleep when it was obvious Logan was long gone. He didn't even wait around for my morning sickness to pass before leaving.

I told myself it didn't matter; as long as I didn't eat anything, then I would be fine. Aside from that, I wanted to leave the woods with a clean body. I was sure he wouldn't mind me using the lake one last time.

I made my way to the lake; the gentle rustle of leaves underfoot and the soft murmur of the breeze through the trees provided a comfort that I knew I would miss. The cool water beckoned invitingly, promising relief from my sore muscles and a moment of respite before my departure from the woods.

Stepping into the crystal-clear water, I allowed myself to sink beneath the surface, the cool of the lake enveloping me like a comforting embrace. I surfaced and let out a contented sigh, relishing the sensation of weightlessness and the gentle caress of the water against my skin.

Closing my eyes, I let my mind and hands wander over my body, reflecting on the changes that had taken place within a short period when I'd realized I was pregnant. The subtle shifts in my body, the almost unnoticeable swell of my belly, the soreness of my nipples, the heaviness of my breasts, and the slight widening of my hips.

The morning sickness and loss of appetite weren't excluded; all the changes made me feel a profound sense of connection to the tiny being nestled safely within my womb.

I slathered myself with the fragrant soap I had brought with me, the one Logan had given me in a thoughtful moment. I had always tried to be frugal with it since I didn't know when I would be leaving, but now that I did know, I allowed myself to lather fully.

I couldn't help but marvel at the miracle of life and the strength of the maternal instinct that coursed through my veins. I reaffirmed my commitment to nurturing and protecting the precious life that had taken root within me, regardless of the challenges or the problems Logan and I may have.

Logan's silence on the matter of the baby began to weigh heavily on my heart again despite my vow, casting a shadow of uncertainty over my plans for the future. Had he truly accepted that I would be leaving, assuming that I would handle everything on my own?

The thought sent a pang of sadness coursing through me, mingling with the bittersweet realization that I would soon be leaving behind the solitude and solace of the wilderness that had become my sanctuary.

But as I gazed out across the calm expanse of the lake, I found solace in the knowledge that no matter what the future held, the past month had been the most beautiful part of my life, and he'd given me something so precious that I couldn't hate him.

I remained in the lake for as long as I could and only stepped out when the chill was starting to get to me. I toweled off, noting with pleasure that the nausea had settled down, and I felt fine at the moment. I hurriedly dressed in the clothes I had worn the same day when I lost my way.

I felt refreshed and invigorated by my final bath. As I made my way back to the cabin, I was met with a sight that took me completely by surprise. There, by the entrance of the cabin, stood Logan, belongings neatly packed and arranged. I wondered if they were for me.

But I reasoned that they couldn't be because the only thing I had brought with me was my camera, which made me wonder what he had packed up. I shook my head, wondering if he was planning to go somewhere because I couldn't believe he would be going with me. It was too much to hope for.

For a moment, I stood frozen in disbelief, my heart pounding in my chest as I struggled to comprehend the significance of his actions. I wanted to ask if he had truly made the decision to leave the solitude of the woods behind and return with me to civilization.

The thought washed over me like a wave, making me feel light-headed and weak in the knees. There were so many questions I could ask, but I found myself at a loss for words, overwhelmed by the depth of emotions swirling inside me.

No, I wouldn't be doing any talking for him. I'd done plenty of the talking, and he had remained silent for an entire week; this was the time for him to step up or remain silent forever. Even if he had made his decision, there was no way I was going to make things easy for him.

I ignored him and the things he had packed, went inside the cabin to pick up my camera, and gently placed his borrowed shirt on the bed before stepping out again.

I couldn't help looking in his direction, and neither could I help but notice the uncertainty etched into Logan's features. His usually steady gaze now flickered with doubt, his brow furrowed in deep contemplation.

If anything, I would have to bid him goodbye. As I approached him slowly, I felt a pang of concern tugging at my chest. The sight of him, standing with a troubled expression, sent a ripple of unease through my senses. I longed to reach out, to offer him the comfort and reassurance he so often had provided me, but I held back.

His eyes, usually so steady and sure, now betrayed a hint of vulnerability that struck a chord within me. I could sense the weight of his thoughts, the burden of indecision that weighed heavily upon him. It was as if he stood at a crossroads, unsure which path to take, and the weight of that decision bore down upon him.

I felt a surge of empathy and would have loved nothing more than to draw him into my arms and soothe him; instead, I looked up at his towering height and smiled.

"Thank you for everything, Logan. I'll be leaving now."

He swallowed hard but didn't say anything, and I nodded again; that was his last chance. I slung my camera over my neck and turned on my heels. I noticed he bent to gather his backpack and another bag which he carried across his chest and started to follow me.

I turned back, "No, Logan. You don't have to see me off; I'll find my way out. I know the path that brought me here." I didn't. I had, in fact, gotten lost.

I expected him to say he was just seeing me off or he was following me out, but still, he remained infuriatingly silent. Okay, two could play the game.

I remained silent as I began to walk, and he began to follow. But as we walked deeper along the forest path, Logan's behavior underwent a jarring transformation that took me by surprise.

It was as if a switch had been flipped, and he went from being distant and reserved to suddenly hovering over me like an overprotective guardian. With every step I took, he was there, fussing and fretting as if I were made of delicate glass.

He would reach out to steady me on uneven terrain, his hand lingering on my arm longer than necessary, as if afraid I might stumble and fall at any moment. His sudden display of care and concern grated against my nerves, setting off a whirlwind of conflicting emotions within me.

On one hand, I couldn't deny the warmth that blossomed in my chest at his attentiveness, the way his concern felt like a soothing balm after weeks of silence. But on the other hand, it felt suffocating, like he was trying to wrap me in cotton wool and shield me from the world.

I couldn't help but feel frustrated by the sudden shift, the stark contrast between his previous demeanor and this newfound protectiveness. It felt like he was overcompensating for something, though I couldn't quite put my finger on what.

When he reached out to steady me on a particularly uneven patch of ground, I couldn't hold back any longer. "Logan, what's gotten into you?" I snapped, my tone sharper than intended. "You've been distant for weeks, and now you're acting like I'm incapable of taking a single step without your help."

My words hung heavy in the air, and for a moment, Logan looked taken aback by my outburst. But instead of backing down, he simply sighed, his expression a mix of frustration and concern.

□His silence hung heavy in the air, casting a new light on our strained relationship. I stood there, rooted to the spot, unable to tear my gaze away from him as his sigh echoed in my ears.

□I was tired of him remaining silent and acting like a victim. I whirled around on him, "Go away! Why are you here anyway?

Why are you following me?"

I sighed when he remained silent again. "I really don't want to see you. Please go!"

"I can't!" he said suddenly when I least expected him to speak. "I'm here and following you because I love you! You can't just tell me to leave."

"What? You love me?" I repeated. My voice was barely a whisper, and disbelief colored my words.

Logan nodded, his expression earnest and vulnerable. "I do, Elena. I've loved you for longer than I care to admit. I want to be a part of the baby's life."

The weight of his admission settled over me like a heavy blanket, wrapping around me and threatening to suffocate me with its intensity. It was a revelation I hadn't seen coming and yet, somewhere deep down, I couldn't deny the flutter of warmth that stirred in my chest at his words.

"What?" I repeated dumbly, my voice trembling with emotion.

He nodded again, his eyes never leaving mine. "I want to be a part of their life, Elena. I want to be there for you, for both of you."

His words washed over me, filling me with a strange mixture of hope and apprehension. Part of me wanted to believe him, to trust in his sincerity, and to allow myself to hope for a future together. But another part of me remained wary, haunted by the memories of his past silence and the walls he had built between us.

"Why were you so standoffish, then?" I pressed, unable to suppress the lingering hurt and frustration that simmered beneath the surface.

Logan's gaze faltered for a moment, a shadow passing over his features. "I was afraid," he admitted, his voice barely above a whisper. "Afraid of losing you both."

"What?" I repeated for the third time. Out of all the reasons I was expecting, that wasn't among them.

17

Logan

"Afraid?" She sounded like it was the most insane excuse she'd ever heard, but where should I start?

"Yes, Elena. I was afraid you were going to attract the curse that follows me around. I was willing to let you go to protect you. But I couldn't let go anymore, not when you're carrying my child."

She sighed and looked almost exasperated. "What are you talking about? A curse? In the 21st century? Come on, Logan."

Yeah, she probably wouldn't get it, but I was ready to help her understand. "Yes, a curse. Do you think I wanted to stay for months on end inside the deep woods with no one to keep my company? Do you think solitude was so enjoyable that I would leave everything that mattered behind?"

I was getting angry, not at her, but at myself, at fate, and my darned curse. "Did you think I didn't love you when I asked you to leave once your leg healed? Did you think it would be easy to let you go? Do you think I felt good not being able to show the joy and excitement that filled my heart when you told me you were pregnant?"

My voice rose until I was shouting, "Yes! A curse in the 21st century. It definitely exists."

"Logan..." She reached out to touch me, but I stepped back, unsure that I wouldn't collapse if I allowed her comfort.

"The curse is so real that I lost my mother, father, ex-girlfriend, and the comrades I went to war with. I lost every last one of them, and I didn't want to lose you. You mean too much to me; I wouldn't survive without you."

I didn't realize the tears were streaming down until I felt them slide across my face; I dashed them away furiously. "Does everything make sense to you now? Do you see why I can't hold on to you?"

"Let's calm down, Logan. I can only understand what you're saying if you explain calmly." She tried to guide me to the nearest tree. "Sit with me so that I can understand you."

"You can sit." I felt too agitated to sit. She nodded and sat down, looking at me curiously.

Opening up to Elena felt like peeling back the layers of my soul, each revelation a step closer to uncovering the depths of my pain and suffering. But I knew I had to share my truth with her; no matter how difficult it might be, she had the right to know.

"I've been through more than I care to admit, Elena," I began, my voice trembling slightly as I braced myself for the flood of memories that threatened to overwhelm me. "I've endured hardships that have left scars on my soul, wounds that may never fully heal."

"My mother, she died right after she gave birth to me, and I grew up hearing different people say I killed her just so I could live. My father didn't agree with them; he always told me how much she loved me right from conception. You see, it took almost ten years after they got married before they could conceive."

"When the chance to pick between mother and child came up, my mother willingly sacrificed herself. My father always said how similar we looked and did his utmost to be a father and mother for me."

"But my father," I continued, the memories of his battle with cancer flooding back with painful clarity. "He was my rock, my anchor in a stormy sea. It came as a shock when cancer took hold of him; he had been too busy mourning my mother and taking care of me to look after himself."

The tears were coming unbidden now, and I didn't try to stop them. "I was eighteen when it happened, and it spread so fast that he was given just three months to live. I watched as he withered away before my eyes, his once-strong body reduced to little more than a shell of its former self. I wasn't even there when he passed on finally."

"People spoke at his wake and burial; some tried to comfort me, but others said I'd killed him the same way I killed my mother. It was so awful, but it was bearable because I knew they were right."

"Logan…" She tried to interrupt but relented when I raised my hand.

The ache in my chest was almost unbearable as I spoke, the wounds of his loss still fresh and raw despite the passage of time. But I pressed on, determined to share my truth with her, no matter how much it hurt.

"And then there was Willow; I met her right after my father died." I continued. Her name was a bittersweet melody on my lips. "She was the light of my life, the one who brought warmth and joy into even the darkest of days. I thought I would have a second chance with her, and she would be with me forever."

I could feel the tears welling in my eyes as I spoke of her, the memories of our time together flooding back with overwhelming intensity. But I knew I had to continue, to share with Elena the depth of my pain and sorrow.

"But she was taken from me right on the day I wanted to propose to her," I said, my voice barely above a whisper. "In an instant, she was gone, leaving me alone in a world suddenly devoid of light and warmth. It made me realize that I wasn't lovable and I didn't deserve to have anyone around me."

The pain of her loss was still fresh, the wounds still raw like it happened yesterday. But as I looked into Elena's eyes, I saw something there that gave me hope, a glimmer of understanding and acceptance that warmed my soul like a ray of sunshine breaking through the clouds. I didn't dare relax, though.

"I've been through hell, Elena," I confessed, my voice choked with emotion. "I tried to take my life afterward, to no avail; it was like death was taunting and teasing me. It felt like I was invincible to death, and fate only targeted people around me."

"Before I came here, before I found solace in the wilderness, I was..." I paused, searching for the right words to convey the depth of my pain and guilt. "I mentioned that I was a soldier stationed at the front lines of a war," I continued, my voice growing quieter as memories of that dark time flooded back.

"But the truth is, I signed up to be a soldier and to be at the front lines after I couldn't commit suicide. I thought I would be easily killed there, but months passed, and nothing happened. Then, I thought I was invincible and that nothing could touch me," I said, my tone bitter with the knowledge of my own naivety. "But then... everything changed."

"There was an ambush and then an explosion," I said, my voice barely above a whisper as the images of that fateful day played out in my mind like a gruesome film reel. "A bomb went off, and... I lost everyone."

"I was buried under rubble for days," I continued, my voice hollow with the weight of the memories. "I thought I was going to die alone and forgotten, just like everyone else. But I was unscathed, not at all hurt while everyone else was blown to pieces."

"And that's when I realized..." I paused, my heart heavy with the weight of the truth I was about to reveal. "That's when I realized that I was truly cursed and the best thing to do was to live somewhere all alone. If the curse would catch up with anyone, then it should be with me."

"That's why I'm here, Elena, why I chose to remain in the deepest part of the woods," I said. "To face my demons, to confront my fears, and to keep everyone else safe."

"Elena," I continued, "I've spent so long pushing people away, afraid that my curse would bring them nothing but pain and suffering. But fate had to be so callous; it brought you to me. I think I fell in love at first sight, but I couldn't allow you to be a part of my curse. You're too precious for that."

I took a deep breath. "I thought I could let you go and nurse my broken heart, which was why I've been distant, Elena. For that, I'm sorry," I said, my voice thick with emotion.

"I love you, Elena," I whispered, the words falling from my lips like a prayer. "And I promise to do everything in my power to protect you and our child. No matter what challenges lie ahead, we'll face them together as a family."

"Do you think you can be with me despite all these tragedies? I'm terrified of losing you."

She remained silent for the longest time, "Yes, Logan. I will be with you." She got to her feet. "But I don't think you have a curse, and it's not your fault that those you loved and cherished died. If anything, you're a survivor, and there are purposes for you."

"Let's talk about fate. I think we met for a reason; maybe you're finally being compensated for everything you've lost so far."

I wasn't convinced, and I searched her face unsurely. She said, "Listen, I know there's nothing I can say to convince you, but why don't we take things one step at a time. Don't shut me out, and allow me to show you just how much I plan to stay by your side."

I stepped over the distance between us and held her close, feeling her energy as she strained against me. "I love you too, Logan. It scared me that I would have to leave you behind." Her warmth calmed me as much as the fact that she loved me.

"You love me?"

"So, so much," she confessed, her lips finding mine. I tasted her tongue and groaned, backing her up against the nearest tree. My desire for her ignited, and I hastily tugged her little shorts down to her knees, sinking into her wet heat.

She was ready for me, and I groaned with pleasure as I thrusted in and out, careful not to overwhelm her. "Fuck, I needed this," I grunted, holding her against the tree and driving my dick inside her. "Hold still, Lena," I instructed, feeling her start to wiggle. "I've wanted you for days."

I moved faster with my eyes closed. Within seconds, my hot release filled her, and I had to catch my breath. I opened my eyes, burying my face in her neck, slowing down as her pussy continued to writhe around me.

I reached up, petting her clit as I promised, "I love you so much, and I'm going to do everything to protect and take care of you."

I gently raised her to sit on a branch of the tree, her feet dangling in the air as I knelt before her. My cum began to drip from her pussy, but I ignored it, using my thumbs to spread her lips. I leaned forward to lick her clean so she could walk freely without my release dripping from her.

I kissed her softly, brushing the hair away from her face and moaning as I thrust a finger inside her. "I will never let you go again." She smiled down at me, her trust in me seemingly unwavering, and I held on to her tightly, grateful that I'd realized what I would be losing if I didn't confess my love. I felt contented and at peace to have her in my arms.

Her moans grew louder as my mouth brought her to climax, and I savored the taste of her pleasure. Neither of us cared that we were in the open.

18

ELENA

I felt deliciously sore in between my legs, but I had no complaints, none at all. The happiness filling me was enough to compensate for any pain; besides, the enjoyment was mutual, and I felt like I could fly if I spread my limbs wide enough.

"So, tell me. How did you end up in the woods?" I heard Logan ask, and I realized he finally felt comfortable enough to ask and learn about me now that he had told me all he had been keeping hidden.

I was walking in front of him, and he seemed to take my internal musing as not wanting to answer him, so he said, "You don't have to say anything if you don't feel comfortable just yet. You waited until I was comfortable enough to share with you, and I can do the same."

"No, that's not it." I hurried to assuage his assumption. "I'm just thinking about how far we've come and how happy I am that you finally feel comfortable enough to ask about me."

"Oh," he said and scratched his head, looking like a cute adolescent. "I thought it was some ugly story that you didn't feel comfortable enough to answer just yet."

"No, Logan. Contrary to what you might think, I had a very happy childhood." I could see his face darken when I mentioned that, but he needed to hear it because I intended to give him the childhood he had missed if he would allow me.

"Do you really think this will work out despite being polar opposites?" He looked almost ashamed, and my heart went out to him; he had so much healing to do.

"Listen, we will. I'm not saying this because I want you to feel bad; I just want you to know me better." I walked backward to lay a reassuring hand on his shoulder.

Logan swallowed hard and nodded, waiting for me to continue.

"I was the only child, and my parents had me pretty late; I came after they'd exhausted all options of conceiving naturally, and they were already thinking about adoption." I smiled to myself; my parents never got tired of telling me the story. "I was told I was conceived on a night when they decided to go wild and try something new."

I could tell I'd captured Logan's attention; he was smiling when he said, "How so?"

"When you meet my mother," I stopped short as I realized I might be assuming things and retracted my words. "I mean, if we ever get around to having you meet her, you don't have to meet her if you don't want to, it's totally…"

He stopped me this time, laying a hand on my shoulder, "Why wouldn't I meet your parents? That's the first thing we are doing as soon as we reach town."

My breath hitched, and I sighed in relief, unable to stop the happiness that blossomed in my chest. We had yet to speak and decide on things, and I didn't want him to take to the hills at the mention of commitment. I didn't want to hurt myself by having high hopes.

"Oh, okay," I said lightly, trying to play things cool. "So, as I was saying, when you meet my mother, you'll realize that we are actually polar opposites. She's so feminine, refined, classy, and sophisticated in a demure way. I don't really know how to explain to you."

"So, that's where you get your elegance," Logan mused, and I was sure I heard him wrong, so I stopped to look at him.

"Excuse me?" I asked, wanting him to repeat what he'd just said.

"Nothing; you can continue speaking, please."

"Yeah, that's what I thought." I do not exist in the same world as elegance. "Anyway, they decided to have a rowdy night and explore their fantasy; the theme was a one-night stand after meeting each other in a club. I still find it hard to believe because my mother isn't club material. She's more of a seven-star hotel guest, private island's frequent visitor… if you get my drift."

I could see Logan was having a hard time keeping a straight face, "Yes, I can definitely picture that."

I nodded, "So, they dressed up and went to a club where they danced with each other. The thought is so mortifying; my mother was thirty-five while my father was thirty-nine. I believe they might have traumatized the teenagers they met in the club."

"Anyway, they went to a motel afterward, and you know, everything happened, and they returned to their normal lives. A few weeks later, after receiving news that they had been pushed back again on the adoption list, my mother realized she was pregnant, and everything else was bliss."

"That sounds very interesting; your parents must be really amazing."

"Yes, they are." I nodded in agreement. "You can surmise how much love I got from parents like that. They never missed any school outing, never imposed their dreams on me; they supported everything I wanted, and I was allowed to chase my dreams. That was how I became a photographer."

"Wow, that sounds amazing." Logan looked wistful and almost envious, but there was nothing I could do about that.

"It's safe to say that I've always known I had the responsibility to make them proud, and I made sure I did just that with everything I tried. I'm always good at whatever I do, and that includes photography."

"That's obvious. I saw your photos, remember?" Logan agreed, and it further assured me that the women were wrong; they probably didn't even know one bit about photography.

"Yeah, only dumb people wouldn't agree with that." I flashed him a winning smile.

"Uh, Elena? I loved hearing about your parents and how you were conceived, but you still haven't answered my questions."

I chuckled. I didn't know Logan was so impatient when it came to conversations, either. I thought he was only impatient during sex. "In a hurry, are we? I was just getting there."

He had the grace to look chagrined, and I laughed again; it was so much fun talking with him. "Well, this might sound a little unrealistic to you, but I left home because of what happened on the day of my first opening."

Logan plucked me away from the path that I'd headed toward without a preamble, carrying me like I was a bag of feathers. "What happened?" he said, without missing a beat.

"I thought you told me to keep going straight; this is left," I said.

"Yeah, we have to take detours now; this is a shortcut," he replied briefly.

"How do you know? I thought you never left the woods." I flashed him a suspicious look.

"Woman," he laughed, "I might have chosen to stay here, but that doesn't mean I don't go out for supplies. I leave the woods once every two months. Now walk; this path is dangerous once night starts to fall."

"Okay," I said and fell silent.

"Why did you stop your story?" he asked after we'd walked a few steps without saying anything.

"Oh, okay. Just before you found me in the woods, I had my first gallery opening, and everything was sold out even before the evening was half over. I was overjoyed and over the moon because I'd had so many doubts before finally agreeing to do the first viewing. My parents encouraged me and assured me the artworks were beautiful."

"I wish I could have seen them."

"I went to the restroom sometime after everything sold out and happened to overhear some women speaking. They thought my work was ugly, and they said many people bought the artwork just to get on my parents' good side."

"What? They must have been jealous; that's the only explanation," Logan answered without missing a beat.

"I didn't think so. I checked for the artwork the women had purchased, and they were some of my favorite pieces. It was safe to say the doubts and insecurities took hold, and I found myself looking for every way to prove them wrong. I left home a few days later to explore further and expand my horizons."

"So, you thought you weren't good enough, right?" Logan asked as we reached a less dense part of the woods. I could easily see in the distance, unlike where we'd been walking and where we could only see trees.

"Yes, and I wanted to prove to myself that the success of the gallery was due to my skills and talent. Not because of my parents' influence."

"Did you check how many works of art they bought? Was it more than ten?" Logan asked, and I wondered how this was related.

"No, they bought three altogether," I answered.

"Now, how many artworks did you display?" he asked again.

"Around eighty," I replied. It was exactly eighty-five.

"Now, did you stick around to find out what the rest of the people who bought the remaining seventy-seven thought?" His tone was casual, but I could tell he was serious.

"No, how is that possible? I couldn't sit them down and ask them one after the other; I didn't even see the reviews before I left home." I was rolling my eyes now.

"That means you don't know the opinions of others aside from those women?" His questions started to grate on my nerves, and my legs hurt since I had walked for close to three hours.

"No, I don't. What's your point exactly, Logan?"

"My point is that you shouldn't have allowed their negativity to get to you. You know that you're good, deep down, so why did you allow them to make you feel lesser than you are? Why didn't you stop to think that the rest of the seventy-seven might have bought the artworks because they truly loved them?"

"Oh." The anger went out of me as fast as it had clouded my mind. "I didn't think that far; I guess I wanted everyone to love what I did and see it the same way I do."

"That's not possible, Elena. But as long as you love what you do and you're good at it, you have no business worrying about their negativity. I love your work, remember? And your parents do, too."

"That's true." I was starting to see his points; he was telling me to embrace my true self and have the courage to face whatever negativities were coming my way.

"You want me to see myself through my own lens and perspective and not what any other person thinks, right?"

"Exactly my point. I mean, I owe those women my thanks. If they hadn't been so snarky, I wouldn't have met you. So, it wasn't totally worthless."

He was right; I was glad to have met him. But I wished I could tell him that I didn't think he had a curse tagging along with him and that I believed fate had just been unkind to him. I wanted to tell him to see himself through my lens and let go of all the burdens he had been carrying, but I knew I needed proof if he was going to believe me.

So, for the moment, I shut my mouth. "I'm really glad I left home and got lost in the woods, too, and that you rescued me."

Logan walked faster so we were side by side and drew me closer to me. "Thank you for coming to me. I didn't think I would be leaving the woods."

In the same way, he didn't know the happiness I planned to bring into his life.

I perked up when I saw a familiar building in the distance, and I realized we were moving closer to the town. It took me a while for the recognition to kick in, and then I remembered the building looked familiar because it was where I'd lodged when I arrived.

"Look! I'm booked into that hotel. They must have been worried sick when they couldn't reach me."

I was pointing excitedly at the back of the hotel, and I saw him smile. "Did they treat you well during your brief stay?" he asked as he picked up his pace so he could meet up with me. I was already running.

"Oh, yes. They were perfect; you could easily mistake them for a five-star hotel. I wondered why the charges were so cheap."

"Really? So, would the services be totally worth it if they decided to increase the price?"

"Of course. I would book it for three times the current price without thinking twice," I replied, my heart swelling with joy as we moved closer to the hotel. "Hold on, why am I discussing hotel prices with you? Do you want to stay here, too? I mean, I have no problem sharing my room."

"We are seeing your parents tomorrow. We won't have to stay for long," he deflected the question.

"Oh, someone is in a hurry," I teased him.

"You're right. I can't wait to see them," he nodded and draped a hand over my shoulder. "Now, let's get inside and get you off your feet; you need to rest."

As Logan and I approached the hotel, I noticed a change in the atmosphere. The employees of the place perked up as Logan and I strode by, their expressions shifting from casual to respectful in an instant. They straightened their postures, offering nods of acknowledgment and warm greetings as we passed.

I almost thought it was directed at me until I watched how Logan effortlessly commanded attention and respect. What did it mean to be with a man who wielded such influence, whose mere presence could elicit such deference?

Logan seemed completely at ease, his stride confident as he greeted everyone with a nod and a smile. I marveled at his ease, his familiarity with this place that was once so foreign to me.

"Welcome, Mr. Powell. I didn't know you were coming. We would have prepared the room."

"It's fine, Phillip. I won't be staying for long." Logan turned around and gestured to the young man who stood at his elbow. "Phillip, meet Elena, my fiancée. Elena, meet Phillip, my assistant. He's in charge of the hotel in my absence."

My eyes widened in surprise as I took in the elegant surroundings with new eyes, the polished marble floors and sparkling chandeliers. It didn't even register that he called me his fiancée. "This is...your hotel?" I asked, my voice barely above a whisper.

Logan nodded, a hint of pride in his eyes. "One of them," he said casually, as if owning a hotel were the most natural thing in the world.

I felt a surge of admiration for him mixed with a touch of disbelief. I had known he was comfortable, but I had never imagined he was *this* successful. And to think, I had stayed in his hotel, completely unaware of his ownership.

"Wow." My head swiveled around. "You didn't mention that you had a hotel."

"How did you think I happened to stay in those woods? Do you think I stumbled upon it and decided to live there? I was able to stay there because I own the entire property."

"Wow," was all I could repeat.

As we went through the lobby, I noticed the way the staff straightened up at Logan's approach, their expressions lighting up with recognition and respect. They greeted him warmly, addressing him by name and offering their assistance with genuine enthusiasm.

"Hungry? We need to feed you proper food."

I couldn't say no to that.

19

LOGAN

If someone had told me a few weeks before now that my worries to come would be about whether my woman's parents would like and accept me, I would have been in denial; yet here I was.

"Come on, they will love you," Elena said for the umpteenth time. We had arrived from the airport and made it to Elena's house about half an hour ago, but I couldn't summon the courage to step out.

All I could think of was all the negative things they could say about me.

"Remember I called them over the phone and told them to expect us? They are probably waiting now. They love it when people are on time."

"So, they hate being kept waiting, right?" I perked up, unwilling to give them anything to criticize in addition to what I already had.

"Who doesn't?" Elena said and sighed.

"Let's go then." I immediately opened the door.

"Really? That's all it takes to make you step out?" She shook her head in amazement as she led the way.

Stepping through the ornate gates of Elena's family estate felt like entering a realm of splendor and tradition. The sprawling grounds were meticulously manicured, with vibrant flowers lining the cobblestone pathways leading to the grand mansion at the heart of the property.

Towering oak trees cast dappled shadows on the lush green lawn, creating a serene atmosphere that seemed to envelop us in its embrace. As we approached the imposing front doors, I couldn't help but feel a flutter of nerves in my stomach.

Meeting Elena's parents was a momentous occasion, one that filled me with a mixture of excitement and trepidation. But as the doors swung open, revealing the elegant foyer beyond, my apprehension melted away in the warm glow of the welcome that awaited us.

Elena's father stood at the threshold, his tall figure exuding an air of quiet authority. His salt-and-pepper hair was impeccably groomed, and his piercing eyes, so similar to Elena's, sparkled with warmth as he greeted us with a smile. "Welcome, you must be Logan, right?" he said, and I nodded, extending a hand in greeting. "It's a pleasure to finally meet you."

I shook his hand firmly, feeling a sense of relief wash over me at his friendly demeanor. "Thank you, Mr. Santiago," I replied, returning his smile. "I'm honored to be here."

"Nonsense, call me Alejandro."

As we entered the foyer, I couldn't help but marvel at the grandeur of Elena's childhood home. The walls were adorned with priceless works of art, while intricate tapestries hung from the ceiling, depicting scenes of historical significance. The air was suffused with the scent of fresh flowers, and soft classical music drifted through the halls, creating an atmosphere of timeless elegance.

But it was the warmth and love that permeated the air that truly captivated me. Elena's mother stood in the center of the room, her graceful figure radiating kindness and hospitality.

Her figure was slender and poised, every movement exuding an effortless elegance that spoke of years spent navigating the highest echelons of society. Her long, flowing gown draped around her like liquid silk, accentuating her feminine curves with understated sophistication.

Her hair was swept up in an intricate coiffure, wisps of golden strands framing her delicately sculpted face. Her eyes, a soft shade of hazel, sparkled with warmth and intelligence while her full lips curved into a gentle smile that lit up the room.

She had an aura of kindness and hospitality that seemed to radiate from her very being. She moved with a grace that belied her years, effortlessly gliding across the room to greet us with open arms.

"Welcome, Logan," she said, her voice like music to my ears. "It's a pleasure to finally meet you."

I now realized what Elena meant when she said her mother wasn't club material.

Her words were filled with warmth, and her smile was genuine and inviting. In that moment, I knew that I was in the presence of a truly remarkable woman—one whose grace and elegance were matched only by her kindness and generosity of spirit. I returned her smile and accepted her gracious welcome.

Her eyes crinkled with laughter as she embraced Elena, enveloping her in a motherly hug. "My darling girl," she exclaimed, pressing a kiss to Elena's cheek. "It's been far too long. I thought you would keep us waiting."

Alejandro joined in the embrace, his arms encircling both his wife and daughter in a gesture of familial affection. "We've missed you, Elena," he said, his voice tinged with emotion. "But seeing you now, with a man by your side, I couldn't be happier."

I watched the scene unfold before me, feeling awed at the depth of love and warmth that surrounded Elena and her family. In that moment, I realized that I was not just entering a home but a sanctuary—a place where love and acceptance reigned supreme and where I was welcomed with open arms.

Elena stepped back after a while and entwined her hands with mine. "Mother, this is Logan."

She turned her attention to me, her eyes sparkling with affection. "So you are the young man who has captured my daughter's heart," she said, her voice filled with pride.

Elena blushed at her mother's words, her cheeks tinged with pink.

"It's so nice to see you; I can tell why my daughter is taken by you." She turned around and gestured for us to follow. "The table is set; please come sit."

As we approached the dining room, my eyes were drawn to the photographs adorning the walls. Each frame held a piece of history, a glimpse into the lives of generations past. But it was one particular portrait that captured my attention—a regal-looking couple, their dignified expressions hinting at a storied lineage.

I couldn't tear my gaze away from the photograph, a sense of recognition stirring deep within me as I looked at the family portrait. The resemblance was striking, the features etched into my memory from countless TV interviews watched in the army, news articles, and occasional mention in society circles.

Could it be possible, I wondered, that Elena came from one of the most influential families in the country? The thought sent a shiver down my spine, filling me with a sense of awe and disbelief. She'd mentioned their influence, but it couldn't be.

Before I could dwell further on my thoughts, Elena's parents joined me looking at the photograph, their expressions filled with curiosity. "Do you recognize anyone in the picture, Logan?" Elena's mother asked, her voice gentle but insistent.

I hesitated for a moment, unsure of how to respond. But as I met her gaze, I saw a glimmer of recognition in her eyes—a silent acknowledgment of the truth that lay hidden within the frame.

"Yes," I replied, my voice barely above a whisper. "I believe I do." Elena's mother was standing beside the present king of Spain.

Elena's father placed a hand on my shoulder. "That's because the woman in the photograph is none other than Elena's mother," he said, his voice filled with pride. "And I am fortunate enough to call her my wife."

I felt a surge of astonishment wash over me at his words, the pieces of the puzzle falling into place with startling clarity. Elena's mother, a member of royalty? Elena is also a princess? It was a revelation that left me breathless, my mind reeling with the implications.

I glanced at Elena, her eyes shining with pride and love. "You didn't tell me you are a princess."

"We didn't get around to it; you didn't tell me you were a young billionaire either," Elena replied with a twinkle in her eyes.

"There must be a lot you're yet to tell each other," Elena's father pitched in. "But while we are on the topic, I would like to know something." He turned to face me.

"Please, go ahead." I gave him my full attention.

"Elena told us she's pregnant, and we would like to know your intentions from the onset."

The warmth and laughter that filled the room earlier seemed to fade into the background as I focused all my attention on Elena, the love of my life, and her parents.

I took a deep breath, gathering my courage as I prepared to speak the words that had been on my mind all evening. "I didn't know the time to say this would come so soon," I began, my voice steady despite the nervous flutter in my chest, and turned to face Elena. "There's something I need to say."

Elena's expression softened, her gaze filled with warmth and affection. "What is it, Logan?" she asked, reaching out to take my hand in hers. "You don't have to answer if you don't want to."

I squeezed her hand gently, drawing strength from her touch as I searched for the right words. "Elena, from the moment I met you, my life changed in ways I never thought possible. You've brought light and joy into every corner of my world, and I can't imagine my life without you in it. This might be too soon to say, but I need you to know that I've made up my mind to marry you. As soon as we are ready."

Elena's eyes widened in surprise, her lips parting in silent astonishment. "Logan," she whispered, her voice barely above a breath.

I took a deep breath and turned to face her father again. "That's my answer, Mr. Santiago. I intend to marry your daughter," I said, the words tumbling out in a rush.

The room seemed to hold its breath as I waited for his response, my heart pounding in my chest. For a moment, there was nothing but silence as Elena stared at me with wide eyes, her expression unreadable.

And then, without a word, Mr. Santiago nodded. "Very well. That's settled then; let's eat."

Both parents turned on their heels and walked toward the dining room, but Elena ran into my arms.

"I love you, Logan."

Tears pricked at the corners of my eyes as I held her close. Elena's eyes sparkled with joy and love; I knew that I would never be able to let her go.

I gently cupped her face, my fingers tracing the delicate curve of her cheek as I leaned in closer, my heart pounding in my chest. Elena's breath hitched as our lips drew nearer, the space between us electric with longing and desire.

And then, finally, our lips met in a kiss that was as sweet as it was passionate—a kiss that spoke of love and longing, of promises made and vows exchanged. Our bodies pressed together in a tender embrace, and the world around us faded into insignificance as we surrendered to the moment. Our hearts beat as one, and our souls were entwined in a dance as old as time itself.

"Dinner is getting cold," Elena's mother's voice came and interrupted the moment.

We finally pulled away, breathless and exhilarated; I knew that this kiss was just the beginning of a lifetime of love and happiness together. With Elena by my side, I was ready to face whatever challenges the future held, secure in the knowledge that our love would always guide us home.

Elena's cheeks were bright pink and flushing madly.

Epilogue - Elena

The last trimester turned out to be a herculean task; I was always eating, sleeping, and getting fucked. It was all I lived for, and I never got tired of it once; being well-fed and properly fucked was the only way I could sleep through the night and get some relief from the Braxton Hicks contractions.

After Logan fed me enough food for three people the night before, and fucked me three times consecutively, the sex was so hard and perfect that I expected to wake up at noon the next day.

But as the dim glow of the early morning light filtered through the curtains, I was jolted awake by a sharp, period-like pain piercing low in my tummy. I winced, the intensity of the sensation surprising me; it was way stronger than the false contractions I had been experiencing.

Sitting up slowly, I tried to breathe through it, hoping it was just a one-off. But the ache persisted, and I knew better than to ignore it. Rising quietly so as not to disturb Logan, I shuffled to the kitchen and put the kettle on.

The familiar ritual of making a cup of tea brought a semblance of normalcy to the surreal sensation building within me. Cup in hand, I settled onto the sofa and tried to dance through the pain.

Yes, I was a heavily pregnant woman waddling in the living room at five in the morning. I'd come to realize that pregnancy makes you do strange things, so I wasn't fazed; instead, I focused on the soothing, repetitive motions of making my body respond to my command.

The quiet of the early hour was punctuated by another sharp cramp thirty minutes later. This one was more insistent, a prelude to the rhythmic tightening that followed. I glanced at the clock, noting the time, and swapped dancing with my yoga ball, bouncing and trying to keep the movement going. The cramps began coming at regular intervals, each one a little stronger, lasting a little longer.

An hour later, the contractions were unmistakable and regular. I knew it was time to wake Logan. With a calmness that surprised even me, I made him a cup of tea and gently tapped him until he opened his eyes.

"The contractions are close," I said, my voice steady. I had always wondered how my birthing episode would go since we chose not to draw up a birthing plan and go with the flow instead. I expected frantic rushing and panicking from both of us, but nothing of the kind happened - maybe because we were more than ready to meet our child.

Logan sat up, sipped his tea, and asked calmly, "How can I alleviate your pain?"

I couldn't speak as the ache deepened into something more akin to pain. "Can you draw up a bath? The warm water might help," I said when the pain eased enough for me to speak.

The pressure in my lower body was intense, and standing around only made it worse. Logan helped me into the bathtub when he was ready and sat behind me in the warm water, massaging my back anytime a contraction hit. The relief from the massage was minimal, and it served more as a distraction than a solution.

We managed to retain the warmness in the water with a heater for as long as we could, but by nine o'clock, sitting in the water no longer helped; by ten o'clock, we managed to put a call through to my parents to keep them updated.

The contractions were stronger, more insistent, and very low. Logan was starting to look afraid as he tagged along with me everywhere in the house. My breathing had shifted to the deep, rhythmic, in-and-out method I'd seen on TV – in through the nose, out through the mouth. It helped me feel in control.

"Let's go to the hospital. I hate seeing you in pain; you can get an epidural."

I was torn, I was ready to go to the hospital, but at the same time, a wave of emotion hit me. Tears threatened as I considered sitting through an hour's drive from home to the hospital.

The thought of sitting through these contractions was almost unbearable. But we had to go.

"Yes, I must be around six centimeters dilated, so we shouldn't stay for much longer."

I waited while he pulled out the car and carried the hospital bag before coming back inside to carry me out. He seemed to understand my pain, and by the time he helped me into the car, I saw that he had plumped the backseat with numerous pillows and a comforter, hoping to make it as comfortable as he could.

I couldn't bring myself to say thank you, not when the pains were hitting back-to-back. Upon arrival at the hospital, my heart sank when the midwife examined me and announced I was only two centimeters dilated.

Two! All this effort, all this pain, and I had barely started. The midwife's calm demeanor contrasted sharply with my frustration. She gently explained that it was too early for an epidural – my body needed more time.

Her suggestion to continue with Logan's back and waist massage and walking up and down the hallway felt like a cruel joke. I didn't need exercise; I needed relief. But, biting back my irritation, I did as told, pacing the corridors and frequently stopping to breathe through the waves of pain.

The next three hours were a blur of increasingly intense contractions. The pressure in my lower body was immense, almost as if I needed to use the toilet urgently; it was intense enough that I feared an embarrassing accident. Desperation clawed at me; I needed pain relief.

Finally, after what seemed like forever, a new midwife administered an injection; the brief sting was nothing compared to what I was feeling. The relief was almost immediate. For the first time since early morning, I could sit. Exhausted, I lay down and drifted into a restless sleep.

I awoke at two in the afternoon to a sudden, astonishing release of pressure. Warmth spread between my legs, and I realized that my water had broken. The brief respite the injection had provided vanished as the contractions returned with renewed ferocity, coming every two minutes, more intense than before. Fear crept in for the first time.

With every contraction came a bit more fluid, making my underpants even wetter and confirming that labor was progressing rapidly. After a while, the need to pee was intense, so I got up and almost fell face down the minute my feet touched the ground.

Logan was hovering around me and was quick to catch me. The walk from the bed in the private room to the en suite toilet felt like a daunting task, and the need to remove the flimsy gown I had on was overwhelming.

"I'll just carry you," Logan said after looking at me for the longest time.

He carried me easily, placed me on the toilet seat, waited until I was done, and carefully rinsed me off. We returned to the room to find the midwife waiting to check on me.

I was now four to five centimeters dilated, still so far from the ten-centimeter goal but prepped enough for the epidural.

My midwife escorted me to the delivery suite to meet the anesthesiologist with Logan by my side. He was lovely and supportive; he spoke in a warm, comforting voice and reassured me that I would be all right. I knew he was doing his best to keep me calm because I was seriously scared.

I no longer felt in control of my breathing, my bowels, or my emotions, and I didn't like it.

Once in the delivery suite, things seemed to move very quickly. The pressure below was burning, and I found it hard to stay still.

The anesthesiologist was trying to explain what he was going to do, but I really didn't care; I just wanted him to get on with it. No sooner had they put a drip in my hand than I felt the urge to push.

I looked down and saw drops of blood on the floor, and my hands squeezed strongly around Logan's in panic. I wondered if the baby was okay.

"Are you okay? How do you feel?" the midwife's voice came, noting my discomfort.

"I need to push. But I can't be ready, right? You said I was only five centimeters dilated." My eyes were searching hers for any sign or clue of something being wrong.

"Here, let me help you sit; let's give you the epidural." She shifted my hips right to the edge of the bed so the epidural could be administered. But the need to push intensified further and I started to get scared.

"I really need to push," I whispered fearfully. The midwife raised her eyes and noted my discomfort before lifting my gown, and from her expression, I knew there was a change in plan.

"What's wrong?" my voice came out shaky.

"Is she okay?" Logan asked from my side.

"You can leave now, Doctor," she announced, and everyone but Logan left the room. "You're fully dilated." She finally answered my question. It seemed that the walk from the labor ward to the delivery ward definitely accelerated things.

This was it. It was the first time I'd actually thought about it. I was going to give birth to my little human. I was going to be a mom... it was finally happening!

The midwife turned me around until I was leaning over the bed, my ass in full view, and I started to push.

The urge was so strong that I kept running out of breath. With each push, I felt a burning sensation in my pussy that made me feel like I was tearing in two, so I stopped pushing.

Then it happened. The one thing I had been dreading throughout the whole pregnancy, the one thing that I had never spoken about for fear it might actually happen. I felt an involuntary release and knew instantly what had occurred. I had pooped. Right there in front of Logan, the midwife, and anyone else who might have been around. I felt a wave of embarrassment wash over me, but it was quickly overtaken by the urgency of the next contraction.

My midwife was unfazed, calmly cleaning up while reassuring me that it was perfectly normal. Logan remained incredibly supportive, telling me I was doing great and to keep going. His encouragement, though kind, was barely registering as I focused on the overwhelming task at hand.

The burning sensation continued with each push, a searing pain that made me feel like I was being torn apart. I kept stopping, fearing the pain, but they kept urging me to push through it.

I gripped the sheets even tighter, my knuckles turning white, and I bore down with all my might. The pressure was immense, and I could feel the baby moving down. The midwife kept coaching me, telling me to push into my bottom and to use the contractions to help guide the baby out.

Each push felt like an eternity, the burning sensation reaching a crescendo before ebbing slightly in the brief moments between contractions.

Finally, after what felt like an endless cycle of pain and effort, I felt a sudden, intense release of pressure. The midwife exclaimed that she could see the head, and I was almost there.

With renewed determination, I pushed again, harder than before. The burning intensified, but I knew I had to keep going. I focused on the thought of meeting my baby, of finally holding them in my arms.

With a final, tremendous effort, I felt the baby's head emerge, followed quickly by the shoulders and then the rest of their tiny body. The sensation of release was overwhelming, and I collapsed back onto the bed, gasping for breath, tears streaming down my face. The midwife swiftly placed the baby on my chest, and I looked down at the tiny, wriggling form. A rush of emotions hit me – relief, joy, exhaustion, and an overwhelming sense of love.

Logan was beside me, tears in his eyes as he looked at our baby. We were both speechless, just staring in awe at the new life we had brought into the world. The midwife busied herself with the afterbirth, but I was barely aware of it, completely absorbed in the moment.

I held our baby close, feeling their warmth and tiny heartbeat against my skin. It was surreal, knowing that this little person had been inside me, and now they were here, real and alive.

The room seemed to fade away, and it was just the three of us – Logan, our baby, and me. We were a family. The pain and the fear were forgotten in that instant, replaced by an overwhelming sense of completeness. Our baby let out a tiny, wailing cry, and I felt a surge of protectiveness and love like nothing I had ever experienced.

The midwife congratulated us and helped us clean up, her warm smile a comforting presence. She reminded me to breathe, to take it easy, and to just enjoy the moment. I nodded, still in a daze, my focus entirely on the tiny miracle in my arms.

I marveled at the tiny fingers and toes, the little nose, and the soft tufts of hair. Logan kissed my forehead, and I leaned into him, feeling a profound sense of gratitude and love. We were exhausted but exhilarated, our hearts full. The journey had been long and hard, but it had brought us to this incredible, life-changing moment.

"It's a girl," Logan said. "I told you I wanted a mini-you."

"Well, you did," I smiled.

"I love you so much, Elena."

"I love you too," I replied.

"Listen, I've wanted to tell you this, and I've been carrying this around since the moment I told you I was going to marry you in front of your parents." He withdrew a package from his pocket and showed it to me. "In truth, I was waiting for the perfect moment, but I hesitated when you said you didn't want to rush things between us, and you didn't want us getting married when you were so huge."

"Logan..." I knew where he was heading already.

"I can't seem to find a better time or moment. I want to ask you to be my wife in the presence of our baby. Will you marry me, Elena Santiago? And be the mother to all my kids and spend the rest of our lives together while I continue to love you with everything in me for as long as I breathe?"

"Yes!" I said softly. The sense of fulfillment that filled me wasn't because we had finally gotten around to saying yes to forever but because I'd successfully helped him understand that he carried around the biggest blessing.

He didn't have a curse; life had been unfair to him, and he had finally been compensated with everything good. It would continue to remain so.

"Yes, Logan. I'll be with you until death do us part," I repeated firmly. "I finally thought of a name for her."

"Really?"

"I would love for her to be called Lowen." I looked at him. "Lowen Powell Santiago."

"My mother's name?" Logan gasped in surprise.

"Yes, I love it so much; it's so perfect."

He finally slid the ring on my finger. "I'll love you forever, Elena Santiago Powell."

THE END

If you loved **The Broken Mountain Man** *then you will love* **Longing for my Billionaire**.

(Click here to get Longing for my Billionaire)

Felicia walks in on a shocking truth; her fiancé is in their bed with another woman. She's shocked, but not surprised. Although she's hurt, she takes the revelation as a sign to follow her heart back home to New York for a fresh start.

Marc Joesphs, a billion-dollar man with even more expensive taste, has been at the top of his career for years. He owns a luxury car dealership that breaks the bank every year. He's got it all. The only thing he doesn't have in his life is someone to love. Someone who can keep up with his sex drive and make every day feel brand new.

Things change when Felicia comes home from New York. There's a spark between them that neither of them can ignore. The only problem is, she's his best friend's sister and she's twenty years younger than him.

They each give in to their temptation and start to sneak around. Kyle, Marc's son, has grown a liking to Felicia himself and when he realizes what's going on between her and his father, things take an even more interesting turn.

An unexpected pregnancy complicates things even more.

Will they come clean to her brother, and will she stick it out with the man she fell in love with?

This Off-Limits Brother's Best Friend Romance will have you panting for more. Read the prologue and chapter one on the very next page!

Sneak Peek

Sneak Peek of Longing for my Billionaire

Who's the brooding billionaire with the sleek, black Aston Martin?

Oh crap...

My brother's best friend and boss is more irresistible than ever.

Walking in on my ex-fiancé with another woman was the final straw.

Returning to New York seemed like a fresh start.

But then, I met Marc Josephs.

All six feet of dominant, dark-haired temptation.

He's my brother's best friend and twenty years my senior.

The way he commands a room, the way he loves his son...

I never stood a chance.

Sneaking around with Marc is risky.

But the biggest secret of all...I'm carrying his child.

(Click here to get Longing for my Billionaire)

Prologue

Marc's hands gripped both of my breasts, squeezing them tightly. His tongue swirled all over them, making me arch my back with pleasure as I rode him. Never in a million years did I think I'd actually get a chance with him. No one ever knew, but I'd always fantasized about him pleasuring me.

"You're so perfect," he said, gripping my hips while I rode. "Perfect in every way."

His sweet little nothings meant the world to me every time we had sex. His voice was so sexy, so firm and deep; it made me ooze with goodness every time he spoke to me. If we got caught doing what we did behind closed doors, we knew we'd be in for a world of trouble. But we didn't care. All we cared about was making love to each other so passionately that neither of us had eyes for anyone else.

"You feel so good," I moaned. "Better than any man I've ever had."

"And you feel better than any woman I've ever been with," he said. "Your warmth and wetness squeezing me makes me never want to let you go."

All it ever took for me to climax was for Marc to place his hands on my lower back and pull me close to him. My guilty pleasure was so dark and troubling, but I couldn't give it up. Even if it meant ruining a relationship I'd known most of my life.

Our rendezvous went on while my brother and a slew of people were in the next room, enjoying his company party. No one knew we'd snuck away to have sex in an unoccupied storage room. I'm sure Kyle, Marc's son, suspected something. But even he was too preoccupied with what was going on inside the party to notice. So I thought.

Instead of ending our sex fest after I came all over his throbbing shaft, Marc lifted me in his arms and pushed me against the wall. He pounded me so hard I thought we'd fall through the floor and everyone downstairs would catch us in our most intimate act, but he slowed his pace when he remembered where we were.

"You drive me so crazy," he moaned. "I could do you like this all night."

"I know, baby," I moaned. "Me too."

I felt him reaching his peak and started to nibble on his earlobe. He loved that. Just as he started to ooze his own goodness, I wrapped my arms tightly around his neck and accepted every ounce of it that he gave me. It was so warm inside me, like a cup of joe on a cold day. I wanted more of him, but we'd already pushed our luck long enough. We had to rejoin the party before my brother came looking for us.

"You go out first," he said. "I'll come out shortly after. I'll say I was on a phone call that couldn't wait or something."

"Are you sure that'll work? What if someone heard us? We were pretty loud in here."

"Hey," he pulled me in for one last kiss. "Just act natural. No one heard us."

I did as Marc suggested. I felt good, like I got away with murder another time. Then suddenly, my heart skipped a beat. Kyle was waiting at the bottom of the stairs with a sinister grin on his face, wicked enough to make anyone fear him. I had no idea what he wanted or what he was doing there, but I prayed Marc didn't leave the closet any time soon.

"Hey Kyle," I said. "Are you lost?"

Chapter 1

The scent of sex and the sounds of passionate moans drift out of my bedroom as I enter the tiny apartment I share with my boyfriend. Sean has been out of work for a few months, so I figured I'd come home early and surprise him with a night out - something to spice up our relationship again.

I'm confused. My hands tremble as I quietly make my way with each step. I can hear Sean panting and groaning behind the closed door and can only hope he's there with an intruder.

I think of calling out to him, but my voice is caught in my throat along with the many questions clouding my brain. The door is cracked. I can see Sean hovering over a figure in the bed. The minute that figure shows her face, I immediately shout bloody murder.

"Sean! What the hell is going on here?"

I burst through the door and throw my drink in his direction. The cup comes apart and spills all over the bed, and all over his mistress. It's some blonde who looks like a good time. At my expense. I don't think so.

"Shit! Felicia, what are you doing home so early?"

Sean scurries to find his underwear, but I grab them from the pile of clothes at the foot of the bed before he can reach them. I start swinging them at him, throwing slaps and punches at his head.

He's dodging my blows like a pro boxer. When he's able, he grabs my arms and pins them down at my sides so I'll stop hitting him. Now I have to use my feet.

"What am I doing here?" I shout. "What the hell is she doing here? In our home? In our bed! Are you serious right now?"

Whoever his blonde friend is looks like a deer caught in headlights. She's also scurrying to find her clothes, to cover the shame and embarrassment she must feel.

"Felicia, I'm so sorry!" Sean pleads. "This isn't how I wanted you to find out about this."

"Find out about what!" I shout. "Find out that you're sleeping around with another woman? What, are you two planning to run away together or something?"

I feel nauseous. Knowing that Sean has been sleeping with another woman in the bed we share makes me feel dirty and low. Just as I turn to leave the room, I run into another nightmare.

"I was going to tell you," Sean says, sounding sad. "The timing was just never right."

I lift the opened envelope from our leasing office that was laying on the floor near his shoe. It's the termination of the lease.

"You've been planning to leave?"

"I'm sorry, Felicia. I just can't do this anymore."

"And what am I supposed to do? I can barely afford the rent on my own and you were just going to leave?"

His fling is dressed now. She looks just as confused as I am about what's going on. It's clear: this isn't their first time. It's evident that he hasn't been honest with her either. She's looking at me with questions in her eyes, but I have no answers for her.

"Maybe you can ask your brother to help you out again."

The sound of Sean's voice makes me cringe so hard that I feel like throwing something else at him. I've had to ask my brother for money several times because of Sean's gambling addiction. I'm not doing it again.

"Just leave, Sean," I sigh as I walk away from him. "I'm done with this. So pack your shit and be gone as soon as possible."

I leave the bedroom angrier than I've ever been in my life. Although I'm livid, I feel like something inside of me has finally clicked. I've finally accepted that Sean isn't the guy for me. I don't think he'll ever be the guy for anyone, not until he gets his life together. So, this is it. I'm finally done.

"Hey there, little sis. What's up?"

I sob into the phone when my older brother answers my call. I already know he'll say *I told you so.* That's part of the reason I haven't told him much about what's been going on in my relationship. He's made it clear from the very beginning that he hates Sean and doesn't want me dating him. I didn't listen.

"What is it? What's going on?" he panics. "Is it Sean again?"

"I can't do this anymore," I cry. "I'm so stressed. I've been trying to stick it out without asking for your help every time I need it, but I'm over it. I'm over Sean and his cheating. He hasn't been working, and all the bills are falling on me. On top of that, I just caught him in our bed with another woman."

"What?"

My brother never raises his voice, so when he does, I know that means he's pissed. He probably wants to fly out right now and give Sean a piece of his mind. Maybe even smack him around some.

"I've been telling you from day one that guy is no good for you. He's only out for a fun time and nothing more. I saw right through him the minute you said you were moving to California. He wanted to have you all to himself because he thought it'd be an easy way for him to swindle money."

Moving to Southern California with Sean changed a lot of things for my brother and me. He has a billion-dollar construction company but he cut me off financially because I left home to be with Sean. Although life got hard for me, I can't say that I blame him. Jeppe has always been more like a father to me than he is a brother, so when I left home to follow my no-good boyfriend, it hurt him.

"Pack your things," he says. "I'll send a private flight for you tomorrow morning. You can come home and get yourself together without that piece of shit Sean weighing you down."

Reality sets in and it makes me cry even more. I've grown to like the life I've made here in SoCal. My friends, my job, I love it all. But going back home to New York is what's best for me and my sanity.

"Ok, Dad." I joke. "I'll pack up and be ready in the morning. Just let me know what time the flight's coming."

"Ok then," he says sternly. "And after this, I don't ever want to see you with this guy again."

After ending the call with Jeppe, I look up and lock eyes with Sean. He's standing in the doorway of the guestroom with a sad look on his face. His mistress has gone and he wants to talk, but what's there to talk about? How he's a lying, cheating dog who will never be satisfied with any woman he chooses?

How he ruined my life by bringing me all the way to California only to betray my trust and make me want to question any man I choose moving forward? Or maybe he wants to talk about what my brother said, how he only saw me as a meal ticket.

"You're leaving?" he asks.

"I am," I say sharply. "I'm done being your doormat."

He lets out a heavy sigh and hangs his head like he always does. Nothing ever changes for us. I don't know why I ever thought I could marry this guy. I should have left him the first time he stepped out on me.

"Felicia," he says, sounding apologetic. "I never meant for things to be this way for us. I really wanted a different life with you. I just, I don't know, I can't do this right. I know you deserve better."

"I do deserve better. A lot better," I say. "I can't believe I've wasted so many years hoping you'd change, hoping you'd finally grow up and be the man you promised you'd be when we moved here. It was all a lie. All of it. And I'm never going to forgive you for this. Not again."

He stares at me. The seriousness in my tone must have struck a nerve. He looks worried, confused even. I don't know why he'd be confused. He's the one who broke our commitment. Not me.

"I'll be out of here in the morning," I say. "I'm going back to New York to start fresh, and I don't ever want to hear from you again."

"Not even as friends?" he asks.

I can't believe he has the nerve to ask if we can still be friends. Why would I want to be friends with the man who broke my heart? Why would I want to be friends with someone I can't trust? This is just another one of his manipulation tactics and I'm not falling for it again. This time, we're through for good.

"Not even as friends." I stand to leave the room. "I'll start packing my things tonight and by tomorrow morning, I'll be gone for good. I hope you're happy with the choices you made and with whom you made them, because I will never look back from here. You hurt me for the last time."

As I try to walk past him, he gently grabs my hand and holds on for a moment. He's taking in the realization that I'm done for good this time. As badly as it hurts me to leave him and start over, his actions hurt me even more.

"Goodbye, Sean."

I leave the apartment and head for the bar at the corner of our street. It's one of my favorite places in SoCal. My friend, Melissa, works here and she's always coming up with some fancy drink combo that takes the edge off. I'm not necessarily a drinker, but right now, I could use something stiff.

"Hey Fee-Fee!" she greets me with a smile from behind the bar. "Surprised to see you in here today. What's up?"

The second I sit down, she reads my facial expression and knows something is wrong. It's not hard to tell when something is off with me. If my mouth doesn't say how I feel, my face certainly will.

"I need a drink," I say. "It's been a long day."

"I have just the thing."

Melissa whips me up a fruity cosmopolitan and comes around the bar to have a seat with me. She's been my closest friend here and I'm so thankful for her. If it weren't for having her around most days, I would have lost my mind a long time ago.

"Everything alright?" she asks. "You don't look like your normal hot self."

"I don't feel like her either," I say. "I came home early from work and found Sean in bed with another woman."

"Are you kidding me?" Her eyes widen. "That asshole! You're too good to be with someone like him, Felicia. Seriously."

"I know. I'm leaving for good this time. My brother is sending a plane for me in the morning. I just can't believe this. After all we've been through. All the times he promised to change. I gave up my entire life in New York to come out here and be with him because I actually believed we would get married and live the fairytale ending. Wishful thinking."

I feel so embarrassed right now. I know I'm not the only woman who's going through a breakup, but this has happened countless times for Sean and me. At some point, it has to end, and that point is now.

"I'll miss you." Melissa throws her arm around me. "It sucks that you have to leave, but it's for the best. You can't keep weighing yourself down for Sean. He's not worth it. And besides, going back to New York will give me a reason to visit the Big Apple. I've always wanted to see what it's like there."

It is a sad ending in SoCal, but I'm happy to know that Melissa will visit me. I don't have many friends back home and I'm sure I'll be too busy finding a job to make any. I don't know; seclusion might do me some good for a while. I can finally focus on my career and rebuild my confidence after all of this.

(Click here to get Longing for my Billionaire)

Made in United States
Orlando, FL
09 July 2024

48785393R00131